The White Rooms

TP Bragg

Black Cat Distribution

Published and printed by
Black Cat Distribution

TO

Annie and Harvey

&

Family and friends

Acknowledgements:

KSK; MV;PH and especially FAB

By the same author

Fiction

The English Dragon

(Athelney) 2001 (www.athelney.org)

Biting Tongues

(***Black Cat Distribution***) 2005

(www.altculture.org/blackcat/blackcat.html)

Non-Fiction

A Declaration and Philosophy of Progressive Nationalism

(Third Way Publications) 2005

Pending Publication - 2006:

OAK

For information on the author and his works please go to

Black Cat Distribution**:**
http://www.altculture.org/blackcat/blackcat.html

The Beginning

The Catcher watched, narrowing his eyes and squinting out most of the dim light. There was enough credit riding on the fight to rouse his interest - much of that credit being his own. Those who sat near were aware of each of his movements. Nobody sat too close. Nobody talked with The Catcher unless he spoke to them first. Alternately scowling or smiling, The Catcher waited for the white-bodying to begin.

None of them cared for the surrounding weak light or the slight smell of animal blood rising from the arena; though the idea that animals had once been slaughtered for food in that shadowy place stimulated them. Torches flamed against the buildings' walls and around the shaky seating. Electricity rarely penetrated that deep into the town.

Sitting on wooden seats that curved around the centrally marked-out area, faces glowed luminously in the eerie light. Credit/dob/money - had been bet. Watch-outs had been posted and waited in the dark outside. A growing light with its harsh scent of smoke heralded the approach of "the stoners" - the white-bodies. The first fight of the night always carried the most and greatest bets. Pinched-faced boys scurried to collect the last of the dob.

The Catcher leant forward – his lean frame taut. The outcome of a fight was something he could never be absolutely sure of. Certainly he'd been well tipped-off. But he could never get it one hundred percent. That was the excitement. That was how he got his adrenaline to flow. Everything else he controlled. For that was the function of a catcher - to know, to control, to catch. And eventually - of course - to kill.

The torch-bearers entered through the doors at the western side of the cavernous building - then through a gap in the seating and into the arena. Following the flames were the stoners, their faces mute and rock-eyed. All those inside pressed forward, calculating sums in their heads. The Catcher's eyes again narrowed perceptibly. Inside his right-hand pocket he sheathed a bony hand.

The stoners shone incandescently. Each body was guided to its place. The trainers spent their last moments repeating mantras. Mantras not to free the fighters' spirits but to concentrate their earthly minds. The stoners' eyes barely flickered. Each carried the short-sword and the hooked blade - as was the custom (though made illegal many years previously). Visibly The Catcher froze with excitement. Inside his pocket was the hidden, relentless shuffle of his hand's ageing but slender fingers.

Already the stoners' blood was beginning to slow. Catheters had been removed and their bodies plugged. Time was finite and close. "Only the victor would survive!" Time would be compressed - a comet flash in the glowing infinite darkness.

The bell sounded. The white bodies lifted from their chairs next to the arena seats and began to walk clumsily towards each other as if their legs were already stiff. For years they had had to be trained to move their limbs as if the blood still ran freely. And for years the mantras had been drummed into them by their trainers. The whole process carried on for generations - illegally. Years for seconds and seconds for years. Many, many stoners shuttling down the illegal railroad.

The stoners were naked save for white bandannas wrapped around their white-bald skulls. Only a blue or red lightning stripe across the material marked them differently and, of course, a tattooed blue turtle on the chest of the blue-marked one and a red coiled serpent around the torso of the other. In the dark light it was hard to distinguish between the bodies. Yet all who watched and wagered big credit knew their man.

Though their movements were often slow, the effects of their training produced unexpected and rapid swishing of the steel blades; a sharpened edge of a sword or the hooked scythe blade easily ripping open their chalky skin. The Catcher had backed the serpent. But it was the turtle who severed the serpent's hand that carried the arced weapon. Tar-blood gleamed dully and bloody dust fell like pepper to the floor. The congealed stickiness of the direct wound would unplug and lead to the draining of neo-blood. And though this new blood was pumped by a gristly heart, the lack of constant chemicals soon thickened it.

The fighting continued. A gaping gash ran from the blue-turtle's neck to his abdomen. It was almost as if the pain was felt. A flicker in the man's eye betrayed some deep sensation. Was it true that they could still feel pain? How could they feel the intense pain of those horrific wounds?

The serpent slashed again and took off the turtle's nose as the turtle wielded the hooked blade into the red-serpent's thigh. With his other arm the turtle cut deep into the snake's side. Their limbs began to slow in motion and the cuts open dryly. Terror appeared to flash in their eyes as flame-torches were brought close to their white skin. And for all those who watched it was as if the creatures themselves either coiled or withdrew into shell-like armour.

The Catcher looked on and was momentarily distracted from his sums as the terrified serpent widened its mouth. But the snake parried another lunge from the turtle with its handless arm. Though this arm was shortened still further the serpent was able to manoeuvre its body in such a way that with the sword clutched in its good arm it gathered enough speed to swoop through the air. The blue-bandanna, tightened about the skull of the turtle, fluttered through the flamed darkness as the head was sliced clean from its neck.

The serpent sank to its knees. Its job was done. There were a thousand more reds waiting their turn. The fight had been the usual short affair. The crowd was happy. The shorter the fight - the quicker the payout. The red-serpent would go to the White Rooms. He would be spared the worst. Years for seconds - seconds for eternity.

Although The Catcher could never be sure of the outcome he absolutely *expected* to win. The slow motion; the sudden swiftness of the fight; he found amusing. The tearing and renting of the flesh without the thick juice of blood spurting - fascinating (though the diluted, pale neo-blood might indeed flow). Credit would buy favours. From his pocket he brought out the body and legs of his spider; his *rath* – his fingers carefully cupping the beast. For The

Catcher there was work to be done. But first he would collect his winnings. Sniffing the air (which now had a different kind of animal blood charging it) he vacated his seat. Others glanced at him. The arena cleared and was swept ready for the next of innumerable fights.

Leaving the arena through the metal door reserved for his kind (the same markings in each temporary venue), The Catcher turned briefly to see the next pair of white bodies slashing to the death. The Catcher already knew the fate of the slain turtle's body. But the serpent's eyes would witness the signs to the White Rooms. And had they not been told many times of this promised heaven? Wouldn't the victor dream of a life detached from the tubes and catheters of a stoner? A life far removed from the training and the cruelly short end? And yet both men's bodies would be eaten by the acid vats - an undeserved equality.

The Catcher felt little or no compassion. But as was his custom upon leaving he dwelt upon the fate of the fighters and considered whose fate was superior – or hellishly inferior. Would the mind of the victorious red-serpent have time to measure and fully appreciate the terrible trick played upon him? The horror of the flesh-burning liquid perhaps reviving dormant brain cells one last magnificent time? The terrible truth that the White Rooms were not, in fact, to be entered? Or would there be one last transcendental ecstasy of White Pain?

He hadn't time to bet more credit. As a catcher he had to keep low. Higher authorities had interest in him. Breathing in the sulphurous air of the outside, The Catcher reflected upon the real purpose of the White Rooms. How they were kept solely for the children. It deserved the laugh which escaped his blood-infused lips. His right hand again played with the creature in his pocket; his other grasped the credits he had accrued.

Chapter 1

It was at a dinner party that I first became truly aware; drinking too much wine only temporarily deflecting my full and horror-struck attention. Put simply, I was refusing to accept what deep down I already knew. It was, after-all, not something that happened to my kind. I was drinking to forget reality. Drinking to make the smallness of life around me more real - however temporary; for truthfully, I was already beyond the normal and greater world. I had already descended into hell.

'You seem distracted Adam,' came a voice.

'No, no,' I smiled, 'just lost in thought, that's all,' gazing at my wife. Gazing at the surroundings - our so very comfortable surroundings.

'Are you sure you're okay?' my wife asked.

'Yes,' I answered, looking into her trusting, watery eyes; looking at the flowery dress hanging loosely from her swollen breast. Her features were outwardly soft and calm masking a slight disquiet only I could discern.

'You do seem...'

'What?' I barked. The guests stilled briefly - all glancing at me - briefly.

'Are you well, dear? Your face is flushed.' Her disquiet blossomed.

'Too much alcohol,' the first voice boomed.

Always too much alcohol. But it buried the past. Helped me forget. Helped me forget what I had done and seen. Helped me forget how much I had had to lie to her. Staring at the faces I saw only their complacency and contentedness. None of them could possibly know. *Maybe one of them knew.* Maybe one of those guests, one of my "friends" had put the screws on me. Caused my world to fall apart. And each time we threw a party – as was expected of our "rank" – I watched them and listened to their conversations.

Again I studied the eyes of my wife. Nothing was quite real. Studied the faces of the men and in particular their eyes. Who had begun the conversation about spiders earlier – might that be a clue? At last.

As they talked I kept rubbing my big toe; except that I couldn't feel the damn thing. I kept rubbing where it should have been and again I looked at the surrounding faces. Last of all I looked at my wife's face. She was happy – her features had relaxed. She was happy - now. Content also. Life was good for her with a man like me. I was a good catch. Finally. Had a good responsible job. Finally. Reckless perhaps? But a profitable way with credit. I could be counted on you see. Her trust swelled her belly. And I was proud. And I was guilty. And I had tricked her into this false sense of security.

She had overlooked my recent erratic behaviour – but she always did. I kept my job. I smiled at the right times. I tried to forget and not think of another, dirty, desperate world. I tried to fit in. I tried to forget the nightmare. But I couldn't forget the numbness – could I?

The numbness persisted. Its horrific cold unfeeling nothingness – persisted. Rubbing my toes against the inside of the shoe, I wasn't sure if I could feel flesh or not – a brief hope. Panic engorged my heart as I gasped. She looked at me. The dinner party was a "success". Our life was a "success". Promotion was due (would you believe?) and she was pregnant and blooming. Everything was perfect. Nothing could alter that. Nothing could have altered that, but me. And I knew it was all a sham. A *dag* nightmare.

I remembered being introduced to her father, the Commander. An imposing man; a frightening man. Tall, straight, large-boned. Hadn't he fought in the war? Hadn't he led the Legion against the subs' uprising? Oughtn't I to know? None of the subs would have done business with that bastard's son-in-law. But they knew I had money - that I was a somebody. Maybe they knew more about me than I guessed. They must have.

'Have some wine?' inflected a gentler voice.

'Thank you.' Wine kept me sane. Wine. Pure wine.

My wife gave me a disapproving glance. When I drank too much I could go either way. Nodding for approval I smiled kindly, so I thought. I looked deeply at her. Our child was growing in her. I tapped her belly - she became flustered. It embarrassed her. I was ready to laugh inwardly when the panic flushed my face again. This was not a joke; not a dream; not even a nightmare. But neither could it be true. It was as if I existed in two worlds.

Later we stood together at the doorway and wished each guest, each friend, a good night. Perfect. But I wondered about every one of the men as they left with their women clinging to their sides. Patriarchy was the way of our world. Maybe one of those friends knew more about *another* world and about me.

Warm breath escaped in cloudy billows. Our friends hurried to their cars. They were rich enough. All of them, like us, were successful. They would not have been our friends otherwise. As we listened to the sound of the cars rising, watching their lights ignite, I pressed down heavily into the big toe of my right shoe. The wine forced a kind of euphoria through my veins - and also a kind of recklessness. I wanted to tell her. Tell her everything. I wanted to shout out to my friends to come back. I wanted to shock them all. But I would have been signing my death warrant. Or worse. No, I watched the cars pull silently and speedily away - almost flying through the air – between rows of shiny buildings lit up in spectacular light. No - I maintained that dag of a sham.

Hadn't it been a great success? She had asked. Yes. And the word "perfect" almost formed on my lips again.

She led me by the arm back through to the dining room. Things were being cleared away. The eyes of our helpers bored coldly into mine. Could they tell, these lucky ones? Did they know about *her*?

On the bed I sat watching my wife take off the jewellery. I liked the way she concentrated, staring into the mirror. I liked her. I loved her. I loved her in the way anyone could love. It was more than most.

'What did you think about Earnest?' she asked.

'Nothing,' I answered truthfully – I didn't give a holy-fuck dag about Earnest.

'Didn't you notice?' she said unclipping an earring. 'Help me with this,' mouthing her words through her reflection. I undid the clasp of her necklace. 'Nothing?' she repeated.

'That's right.'

She seemed irritated.

'What was I supposed to notice?'

'Why, how jealous he was.'

'Jealous?'

'Exactly.'

I wasn't in the mood for her games. Standing up I forced the blood down into my toes. Why wouldn't the big toe come alive? Why wouldn't the blood circulate? Perhaps it was numb because I had sat awkwardly. When I had spoken to Louise I had had to turn in a peculiar manner. Come to think of it, that was when Earnest made a slight scene with an unnecessary remark addressed to one of the helpers.

'Because I was speaking with Louise?' I said.

'Don't be silly.'

Scrunching my toes and curling them as tightly as I could made no difference.

'Then what?' I shouted.

'For god's sake,' she replied, 'what is wrong with you tonight?'

'I'm tired. There's nothing wrong, I've told you that.'

'Then don't bite my head off. You seem constantly distracted. Earnest was not jealous because you were speaking with Louise.'

Sweat was on the bridge of my nose. 'Then why?' I asked as calmly as I was able.

She rose from before the mirror and went into the bathroom. Water hissed down the pipes. 'Because Louise can't have a baby.'

In bed she kissed the side of my face. 'I love you,' she cooed. 'We're blessed.'

'Yes.'

'We have a lot to be thankful for.'

'Yes.'

'Are you happy?'

'Of course.'

'Why "of course"?'

'Because...' But I couldn't bring myself to complete the sentence. Next to my skin was the belly containing my child. A child that would be born into the Uppers. An Upper. I even hated the crudity of the expression. There was no "up" or "down". Yet only down for me - maybe the child - maybe my wife. Was her world coming to a shattering end? Thankfully she didn't press me for more words as we lay close together.

In the middle of the night I got up and left the room. In one of the guest room's bathroom I sat down on the side of the bath with only a low light for illumination. I sniffed the air for helpers. We believed we could still smell the stench of their previous lives. Out of a cabinet I took a sheathed scalpel. As I sat I considered the routine of the waking day; of going to work and smiling at my staff; of the pretence. It all made sense. That was the unnerving part. It was all so predictable. Taking the blade from its velvet pocket I watched it flash in the semi-darkness. I'd gone down to help one of those bastards. Had I done a good thing? And I'd gone down again. Fool that I was...

Against all the rules I had helped. And been tricked. And I couldn't blame them, or her. I could not blame her. It was all she had. I even think she was genuine to begin with; genuine at the end. But I broke one of the essential rules of life. Simple. But I still could not totally believe - not really and truly believe what was happening. I had had shots for thirty years. There were records showing people who had gone without shots for nearly three years – who remained protected. Were they just freaks?

My mind ached; the thoughts flooding through me caused actual pain. I held the blade close to my eyes. Who had seen what I had seen? Staring down at my big toe I grinned at its ugliness. It protruded ungainly. It didn't deserve to feel. But I did. I had acted out of compassion. I thought I had understood. I thought she had no-one else to turn to. But I had broken one of the rules. And this life had rules.

Bending forward I took the blade and ran it across the skin of my big toe. A great knot of sick filled my throat. The toe split in front of me. No blood ran. The sight of it chilled my good blood. The wound appeared stuffed with gleaming tar. I had to swallow down a ball of acid phlegm. My eyes stared unbelieving at the pared flesh and the blackness shining in the dim light.

A noise outside reminded me of the stealth of the helpers. And of her. And of my wife and child. And it was as if the whole of my life concentrated into a narrowing tunnel of disbelief and fear. The toe gaped up at me. Even a smell rose through the stifled night air. It had only been four months since the last shot. It could not be what it appeared to be. And like a man gone crazy I even remembered Exmass coming. Fucking Exmass. I laughed, dropping a single tear from my right eye almost simultaneously. I was stone cold sober and the blade of the scalpel was shaking in my hand.

The first thing I had to do was hide the sight of the damaged toe; not draw attention to it. At least nobody would be looking for symptoms in me. It was crazy - a crazy nightmare and I had to think fast. The problem was the credit - the damn holy money. If I could get a shot quickly then perhaps I could stem the spread. Only the big toe was affected so far. I ran the blade of the scalpel lightly over the toe that touched the big one. Thank god I could feel the sensation of the fine metal. I was even tempted to draw blood just for the satisfaction of seeing it flow. I had to get credit. It would mean seeing the doctor too. At least I could count on him. At least I wouldn't be on the Register.

Taking some lint from the bathroom cabinet and a roll of bandage I carefully squeezed the wound together. Only then did I realise the stupidity of cutting the flesh open - yet didn't I need to know for certain? With the disease nobody could be trusted. I must have got infected in subearth – of course. Thoughts flooded my brain. I was sweating, not thinking as straight as I should. If only I hadn't listened to her. This is what becomes of the lawbreakers. And this was the way a panicked man thought.

Jo was my main worry. I had to keep everything from her. A sound came from outside the bathroom. I could not raise my voice - I didn't want to wake Jo. Was it one of the helpers? They were my second worry; they would shop me if they could. If they shopped me their life would improve. I thought back to how it had all come about, how a helper had approached me, and how I had foolishly listened. Had she known something about me? I worked for the government, was an enemy to them all. Why had she taken the risk of approaching *me*? I could have uncovered her, had her vaporised - or worse.

But the helper had been beautiful and Jo and I had had problems. It was the beginning of the downfall. We thought a baby would heal us. And the idea seemed to. But a baby (still in the womb) can push a woman to the edge. That's what happened. That's what happened and yet Jo withdrew into her manicured, perfect world…

When I moved through the darkness of our apartment I listened for the breathing of helpers. As I opened our bedroom door I was shocked to see Jo awake and the tableside light switched on.

'What is it?' I asked awkwardly.

'I'm scared,' she replied.

'Scared?'

'Yes.' There was a pause. I stepped towards the bed so that her sight would not be drawn to the bandage around my toe. 'Where have you been? I needed you...'

'What's wrong?' ignoring her question.

'I thought I saw something...'

'Jo?'

'I did.'

'You know that's not possible. You're just remembering the stupid conversation at dinner. It really isn't possible.'

'Why not? One could escape. You've said so yourself in the past.'

'Not here, not in this place - trust me.' How could I have said such a thing? And for a moment I was taken back in time.

'I'm scared.'

'I'll come to bed, turn off the light.'

'Search first. Please.'

'Then you'll sleep?'

'If you search thoroughly.'

I got down onto my knees and looked beneath the bed. Keeping my body between her sight and the bandage, I pretended to look. But there were no spiders. All had been killed. So we believed. The helpers knew well enough how to track and kill them. But then spiders and the disease both existed well enough in subearth - didn't they?

Chapter 2

When I awoke from patchy sleep and spiteful nightmares I momentarily forgot my own dark dread. Jo was asleep next to me and I could hear the helpers tidying around the house – especially the debris of the party. It was in a kind of hazy stupor that my mind raced back. I thought of *her* – the girl – of my real nightmares – of Zee.

Had I paid attention previously to Zee? I tried to wrack my brains. She had been hired through the usual channels and I always got high-security clearance. Helpers were adept at blending into the background. They needed to keep their jobs. Not until Zee approached me do I remember her. And yet she was the most stunning looking helper I had ever seen. I couldn't even recollect Jo causing a fuss. It was possible we weren't even speaking. But then things had eventually gone right. With the "usual" patch up came her "unique" pregnancy. *Except things went wrong too.*

Work had been busy. There was the constant checking of details, the interviews, the appearances in the subcourts (where the subs and helpers were tried) or the Chambers. I hated seeing an Upper go down. And I hated it when a child was taken to the White Rooms. Sometimes it all seemed so unnecessary. But of course it was not.

I remembered Zee. She had tricked me. Caught me just right. But it was the electronic note that clinched it. The note with its code - unmistakable. I couldn't ignore her connection. She also had the most beautiful smile. I suppose I kind of fell for her. A helper. A sub. What was I thinking? But she had the message and the code. That meant someone from my department was involved. Her story could have been true. Must have been true. For the most part - was true.

Jo had been six weeks pregnant when Zee came to me.

'Mr Adam sir?' (It is their way of addressing us.)

'Yes?' I was irritated, had had to bring work home with me. I was lucky to be working in communion still (as the expression goes); lucky to get out of the apartment block. But I had to bring work home many evenings. It was this that sparked off one of the nastiest rows with Jo. But she should have known how privileged we were, even for Uppers.

'May I talk with you sir?'

'Go ahead.'

'In strictest confidence sir?'

Then I noticed her eyes and the shape of her body. This was how she had become a helper, I considered cynically.

With curiosity I answered, 'Very well.'

She sat down, facing me, behind my desk. Her eyes were impassive – softly beautiful. But she was not totally sure of herself. I got up, looked outside the office and shut the door. 'We're alone; speak.'

'I have this,' handing me the e-message. It had the code. Only those working in my department had access to it. I read the screen carefully.

Now that I look back I can see how clever it all was. But they played a chance. And yet it was only the girl that played and took a real chance - to begin with at least. I could have had her dismissed on the spot, even killed, vaporised or worse - sent to surgery. They hated the surgery (it was deeply secret but it happened). But my as then mysterious comrade and this beautiful girl must have seen the opportunity. There was the look of her – a kind of fieriness subdued by self-discipline. There was my baby growing in my wife's womb. The code. Lucky timing? But I wasn't a push-over. There was too much at stake. I did not turn her in. The code prevented that. I said:

'You know what would happen if I reported this?'

She said nothing, but parted her lips slightly. The room was close. On the screen was the file of another young woman. Caught with an Upper and with an unborn child ready for the White Rooms.

'You've taken a risk.' It was an understated remark.

Still she said nothing.

'Wait,' I said firmly. I at least understood her predicament. They knew that. Someone in my department had messed things up. Sure they saw their chance.

That night I could not sleep. There was much to consider. Jo lay peacefully. Things between us were almost perfect. Perfect. The word entered my mind to taunt me. But we were in harmony again. She had even accepted credit from her father to help me out. Sure I got a big wage. But Jo could spend and I gambled with shares. Share-shuffling was the only really dangerous thing I did any more. Until then. Share-shuffling was the way my reckless nature could express itself. I didn't "do" helpers. I told you, I hardly noticed them. Until Zee came along. And Zee was especially beautiful. I suppose I fell in love with her as I had once with Jo. That was reckless enough.

The thing was, I hadn't been getting too many lucky deals. And I'd had to cash in my shot policy. It was no big deal. I couldn't get insurance, I wasn't *that* high-up (to be truthful I hadn't wanted that extra expense), but I could always get enough for a shot - I thought. And I admit credit got tighter when Jo and I fought. She would take it out on me by buying things. Anything. She was a Legionnaire's daughter. She wasn't going to work but she wasn't necessarily going to put up with me and my demands. So her getting the credit from her old man was a godsend. It made life easier for me. I got my job in Records because of him. That's what Jo had always maintained.

So taking work home also meant I could get credit for my shots. Did the message sender know that also? He must have - no point otherwise – no point pounding a blood-less stone, eh? That's why I could have killed him. Killed him with my bare hands. Because he had killed me in a sense; or at least begun to. And he knew. Was prepared to betray me. There had been a serious breach of security for sure.

Something made me decide to trust her. Something made me want to help her To take a risk. A real, reckless risk. Something made me prepared to step outside the laws. And I had never actually been to subearth. Sure I'd seen pictures and flics, but I'd never been *down*. I hated the thought of white-bodying. People were using the illegal fighting as a cover to procure sex-subs; I knew the results of all that. And there was the "supposed" trade in limbs. People said these limbs came from the fighters, but I'd seen limbs that had belonged to women and children. Except we all forgot. We saw and we forgot. Because we only remembered what was "official" and "allowed".

I made an excuse to Jo about working late at the office. Only a worker in communion could do that. My grandfather had done much the same, so many years ago, so our family history told and he had been a wild man. Jo took it. And I was sorry then. Not as sorry as I was to become. We fought a lot, but I loved her. Still love her. Love her more than ever…

The helper just looked so sexy and beautiful. It was as if I wasn't sure of how Jo and I would be. I wanted to be next to Zee that was all. I never did "sleep" with her - I never did "do" her, to use the crude expression. Zee, with her slender pale limbs, perfect curves, hair cut short – dark eyes and her lips a deep, healthy red.

At work I tried to fathom who had been transgressing. Nobody lost their cool. And so it was that on a Mecredi night I met with Zee and we drove towards the border. With the car and my rank we crossed without fuss - it didn't seem surprising to the guards (I remembered their particular border control for future reference). They had wry smiles stuck on their faces. Once across the border the adverts stopped. There were shacks of sorts that soon petered out into rough countryside. The moon lit things up. She didn't speak. She was gong back for the first time for a couple of months. She missed her child; her boy. She felt the tension, so she admitted later. We drove for some time before her town rose upon a hill in the distance.

We couldn't drive in. She knew where to stop. I had to change into the gear she had brought along. There was only me - it was dangerous, and for the first time I felt apprehensive. I was doing something just for the thrill of it; I had nothing to gain but the kick.

Not all the subs had the disease of course. The helpers were screened. There was never any trouble from them because their main hope of avoiding infection came from being out of and away from the squalid subearth towns. But even some of the older subs had stayed healthy.

We walked the last five lengths into the town. The long-huts came into view as clouds scudded over the moon-face. I had seen these things on the screen but only from a distance...I pulled myself up.

'You want to take a look in?' Zee broke her silence – kept from when we had abandoned the car. Her voice sounded different. Why shouldn't it have? Our relationship wasn't quite the same. 'It wouldn't be pretty,' she continued, 'maybe too much. Long-huts are the sepulchers of a strange religion.'

'What?'

'You wouldn't want to look in.'

'No, I want to see.'

She gave me a quizzical look. I'm still not sure if she really expected me to go with her.

A warder sat outside. He paid scant attention to us. There was no reason to. We weren't going to buy. He assumed we were both subs. Apparently relatives sometimes came to visit - might arrive on a windy, moonlit, Mecredi night. The huts were lit only by stoves. The stoves gave their shadowy light and heat. More importantly these stoves stuffed the air with thick smoke, which hid its otherwise acrid stench. How did I know? Close up to the bodies you could smell their perfume.

'They should let them die,' Zee said without emotion, though I thought I detected some hidden feeling beneath her words. I looked at the rows of beds and the naked, chalk-white bodies laid on top. Tubes supplied the mixture which thinned the blood enough to keep it moving. Each had an implant to drive the heart. Waste products were filtered through tubes that disappeared into holes in the hut's walls.

Walking along and sometimes in-between the beds I stopped occasionally to look at the eyes of the bodies. They seemed to stare motionless. But I thought I caught a flicker from a male body, once young and healthy.

'No chance,' said the Warder later.

'What happens to them?' I asked.

'Theyse die,' he said dryly. 'Theyse die eventually. Go to a better place, eh?' he said with a twinkle in his otherwise dead eyes.

'What happens to them then?'

He quizzed me, shrugged his shoulders. But we both knew the answer. Of course I knew the answer. Faced with this reality even I could not *forget* – could not lie to myself.

Before I left, I looked back. There was no sound from them. Just the eyes staring into the metallic rafters of the ceiling. Just the smell of the stoves' fires burning and a kind of rotting odour smelt occasionally. The bodies lay as if dead. But they were alive, and I couldn't imagine how a society could tolerate them being so. And at the back of my mind I registered their full-limbed bodies - their almost unnaturally smooth skin.

I told Zee about how I felt. She thought me sentimental. She went to say something else but stopped herself; then she said: 'Have you ever seen a deformed Upper?'

I had to think, it was something I had never been forced to consider. 'No.' (No I had not seen deformed Uppers because our surgery was so good. That is how we could lie to ourselves.) I felt ashamed but repeated, 'No.'

She laughed.

'Why are you laughing?' Until then I had deliberately not connected the lack of deformities in Upper with the *supposed* trade in limbs. The *supposed* surgery. The *supposed* transplants. Even using the word "supposed" caused me to squirm.

She said nothing and laughed again.

'You think we have no ethics?' she asked eventually.

I could only look. There was too much to consider…to re-evaluate.

'These are the lucky ones. The special ones,' her eyes glinted, 'we let them die in their own time...before...' but she stopped again. I could not meet her stare. 'Did you know that some of these young subs – with their pure skin and pure features,' she looked directly at me, 'come by themselves to the long-huts? Or led by a warder, with a smile on his face?'

I shook my head. There was much I genuinely did not know.

'You think we have no morals. But we subs think the long-huts are a place to escape.' She laughed. 'They, "we", believe the subs in the huts are in limbo – and *they are*.' And she laughed loudly as she said "limbo".

But the huts at least prepared me, however slightly, for what I was to see in the town. Even at night subs were about. Subs with limbs missing; subs with gaping wounds that marked their skins as if grotesque crustaceans had attached; subs with eyes and ears missing and subs as crazy; as possessed; as perverted as anything I had ever seen on the flics. The "unlucky" ones. 'The disease?' I kind of asked helplessly.

'Never seen it up close?'

I said nothing. The bodies in the huts - they were all perfect. I,"we", had never seen anything like that on the flics.

'What happens to them?' I asked tentatively, gazing at the hapless subs.

'You mean you don't know?'

'I think I know,' I replied shakily. As I spoke I also acknowledged the perfection of Zee's form. It was she who was the aberration. And I also realised a complete shift in our relationship. Only then did I have the great desire to kiss her.

'You Uppers,' she began, 'you think you know everything. At least you have everything. At least you have shots.'

My shots would be due shortly. How could I have gambled so much? Even with those figures to haunt me I had taken the ultimate risk. She continued, 'You have no idea what it is to live day to day unsure if you will contract the disease. If the numbness will come. When the brain will start muddling things up. You have no idea what it is to see your mother and father stumbling about, spilling boiling water over their flesh, cutting their fingers accidentally. What it is to hear them ask who you are. You cannot imagine. I am blessed Mr Adam, and so are those bodies you saw lying in the huts. They escaped the real pain. Sure they've suffered. Suffer. This disease is hell, simple. But they have their limbs intact - and for them, no fighting, no illegal chopping.'

'What do you mean, exactly?' I began to say, but at that moment something happened to cut my speech.

Now as I recall what took place I can see the scene in full. There were tumbled down houses filling every narrow dirty street. Fires burning in chimneys and smoke clinging about rooftops. The moon was choked-hidden. Though dark, children raced around - some hobbling. There were fights in "ale" houses; grog houses. Braziers burnt rubbish on street corners. Women with four limbs intact made money from those desperate to feel. To feel one last sensation run through their flesh. But this part of town was where the healthy stayed away, if they could. Even in subearth there was separation.

As I asked for more details about the disease a man rushed up to us, though his gait seemed to throw him forward as if he were out of control. In his hand he carried a long blade. 'It's the devil,' he cried, 'Lord Satan is here. Mock us he. The dark one.' And as I turned my head the blade swept past my face. I could feel its dirty breeze whip across my skin. The man stumbled to the ground. 'It's the angel,' he spat. 'Listen,' he shouted.

'You'll have to shut him up,' Zee shouted. Other bodies were coming from the shadows.

'He's here - the unclean one, hese come.' The man dribbled dirty saliva from his mouth, lifted himself slowly. Bodies had come close.

'Do something, quick,' Zee urged.

I stamped on the man's hand left holding the ground. He groaned. Swiftly I let a kick crack into his face. For a moment he registered no pain. Only his lip bloomed bloodless. Another kick sent him back down to the ground. The bodies around us, a mess of rags and uneven limbs quavered briefly. 'What now?' I said between gasps for breath.

Zee shouted, 'Run!'

Chapter 3

We squashed ourselves into a dark doorway. Zee said, 'It's okay, I think.'

'You think?'

'I'm not known in these parts, helpers aren't liked...'

I looked around. There were some in-tact-looking women subs standing about. It began to impress itself upon me how it might be to live there; existing in a chaotic world inhabited by crazed and diseased people. For the first time I also began to appreciate my good health.

'Come on,' she said at last.

Weaving our way through the dirty streets she led me hand in hand. The touch of her soft skin eased me. Listening intently, I heard strange sounds emanating from the dark dwellings. In the narrow roads ghost-like faces loomed from the shadows; finger-less hands reaching out. At times I swore I could feel the brush of wound-encrusted bodies. All the time I turned my head, Zee spurred me on. She was healthy, a young woman who could easily have fallen victim to the grasping bodies. But she seemed to know the place back-to-front.

'Not far,' she said panting.

Gasping also, I looked into her eyes. Around us fires burnt everywhere.

'It is hell,' she stated.

'You know this part?' I said stupidly.

'Yes,' she smiled, 'I know it. The whole town. Played here as a kid. Played amongst the rats and the crazy ones. Ran away from the old men who tried to catch us. Ran away from the body-snatchers. Nothing changes in this damn place but the eyes in the bodies...'

'The what? You said the body-snatchers?'

'Come on,' she said, 'don't fake it. You work for the government, you must know all about it.'

'About what?' I asked open-mouthed. It was one thing to hear the talk of the people another to hear reality.

She looked at me with her typically quizzically-strained face – her intelligent eyes.

'About what?' I urged.

'Not now,' she said. 'If you truly don't know, you'll find out well enough.'

A figure stumbled up to us. 'Help I,' it said, 'be kind with yer muffer and help I.'

Zee shooed the woman away. The old lady put out her arms to feel for the brick of the wall but they crumpled and she banged her head. I flinched.

'She doesn't feel anything,' was Zee's curt response.

'Them'll get yer,' the old woman sang, 'them'll get yer, have yer limbs off,' she grinned. Her mouth was dark and toothless. She cackled and dropped to her knees, rolled over into the gutter.

'Can't we help her?' I asked.

Zee looked at me with contempt.

Rain began to fall. The guttering from the building shot spouts of water onto the streets. The fires in the braziers were dampened.

'Nearly there,' said Zee.

'Where you live?'

'If you like,' she smiled.

Disappearing down a greasy walled alleyway she pulled me in quickly. 'I don't want anyone to know what's happening,' she explained, 'only those that need to know.'

We entered a broken-down gate and a cat screeched from somewhere in the black back-yard. Zee hissed. The rain falling and mixing with the sulphurous smoke caused the air to feel acrid and acidic. Before the back door of the house she glanced at me. 'I appreciate everything,' she said quickly.

I nodded, unsure how to respond. 'I haven't done anything.'

'But you will,' she almost beseeched.

'I'll do what I can,' and in an instant the former hierarchy was re-established.

Knocking on the door in a particular pattern ensured a light flickered from an upstairs window. I kept glancing into the shadows of the courtyard, expecting to see deformed figures lurking or the scuttling of rats. (It was only later that I was told how the rats would eat to death the bodies who didn't – or rather couldn't - make it to the "dying fields" close to the mass-graves. But people there tolerated the rats - I was unsure if this was for sound or superstitious reasons; or did they eat spiders?) The door opened as rain began to lash down.

A face, a friendly face, took shape behind candle-light.

'It's you,' the face beamed.

'Aye,' Zee replied.

'And this is he?' the face said staring at me.

'It is.'

'Welcome. Come in. We don't lack manners in su (this was the colloquial way they referred to subearth). Quick, afore the rain gets you.'

Inside, I was cheered by the relative tidiness. But a noise from upstairs distressed me. 'Pay no attention,' Zee advised. 'This is my mother,' motioning to the lady who had let us in, 'don't worry, you can see she is disease free. Alive! Most of us are in these abouts.'

Limply I held out my hand. 'Pleased,' I said. Zee stared at me intently. I had expected her mother to be horribly disfigured - if alive at all.

'Pleased,' said the mother, 'greetings and welcome to su.' To her daughter she said, 'I'll get these a drink.' To me she said, 'Youse'll want a drink?'

'Yes,' said Zee for me. 'This is where I am from. Now you see. Not too bad eh? Not quite Upper, then again...We're alive and well, at least. Me being a helper, that's enough for the folks. Mr Adam,' she added.

'There's no point,' I said. 'Just Adam. Just call me Adam. I've seen too much for...'

Again she threw me an acute look. 'You seem to know so little for a government worker.'

She was right. 'I...'

'But you must have seen all the flic-ups (the expression used by the subearths for flics)? Must have learnt all the disease stuff at school and college? Must have friends who go to the white-bodying?' Her questions came relentlessly. 'Must have friends with perfect little babies, eh?'

She was a helper and talking to me this way. But in my arrogance I had not even carried a weapon into the subearth town.

'I've seen things,' I half explained. And I had. Things seen and thoughts buried in my life in Upper.

But she laughed.

'I have come to help. I don't need to do this. You can't assume anything from me.' But the words I spoke rang false.

'I do thank you,' she said suddenly very earnestly, 'believe me. I am yours,' she added. Her mother came in with the drinks.

The mother stared intently at me. Later, when she left (so Zee and I could talk), I asked Zee why she had scrutinised me so. 'Because you're so perfect,' was Zee's response. And I wanted to say something about her form - the beautiful daughter. But. I laughed. 'Tell me about the disease,' I said, 'tell me the truth.'

'An Upper who wants to know the truth?' she asked incredulously.

'Yes.' I also wanted to ask her about my secret colleague, the sender of the e-message and about their relationship. But I knew I could not. I wanted to ask her for many reasons. And as yet I had not even seen the child I was to resurrect.

'The disease?' she mumbled.

'Yes.'

'What do you know?' she asked.

'That it's incurable; that the body goes numb - the brain too?'

'That's it? That's all?'

'We know how bad it is - we think we know. I know that illegal fighting goes on with subs. Every so often we get documentary flics on the portable, and then the government overrides the channels.' I watched her reaction. 'You haven't got much time for Uppers have you?'

She smiled. 'How can you say that? I clean for Uppers; I wash the laundry of Uppers; I get down on my hands and knees for Uppers...' there was a twinkle in her eye. 'I'm risking everything so my child can be brought up as an Upper. And guess what; I even slept with one. That's how children get to be, or is it different in your world?'

'Our world? No. No it isn't different. You know how scarce children are becoming...' And I thought of the White Rooms. Why did we send the children there? Couldn't there be healthy children amongst those sent? There had to be; Zee had a healthy child. At least I supposed so.

'I'll tell you my uncle's story; if you like?'

I nodded.

'We've been lucky as a family - *oh mother, oh father - dear departed, let the moon show his evil face* (this was a saying to prevent bad luck) - but ten years ago, when I was a little girl, my uncle began to notice the numbness. Gradually he began to lose the feeling in his toes and feet. At that time we prayed it was leprosy; can you imagine? I presume you have shots against leprosy too?'

'Yes.'

She carried on, 'But the numbness spread and he damaged his cold foot. At the same time he began to forget things. Only occasionally, you know, not too dramatic. But the numbness crept up his other leg and before long he was walking like a man with clumsy su-made artificial limbs. In this world my uncle had made a living as an auto-scribe (a job which was part secretarial and part copywriter). We try and keep things going, you know. But he lost it. Just as anyone with the disease loses it. So it's the beginning of what we call "the oubliette".

I frowned.

'The start of a prison within a prison. My uncle had to move out of this end of town into the shanty, that's where we came in, that's how I know it so well. My mother never lost touch with him. No hut, no rats for him - she did her best. And I would do things too. That's when I learnt how to get my hands dirty. You have to live with the disease to truly appreciate its horror. Simple things like the way he would sit down and then mess himself without knowing. And how the brain would lose pathways to sense. How he would rub his hands together to keep the feeling. Call me by his wife's name. Descend into the filth and poverty of the shanty. How sores and cuts would gape dryly upon his body. How he began to putrefy. How his brain, his own brain scared the hell out of him. And how in the end he couldn't do anything but take shallow breaths and stare at the ceiling. You know. How his body froze from the outside then gradually froze in the inside and all the while he was losing his precious marbles. And the smell of the dry wounds. The maggots and rats nibbling the body – but they didn't eat him alive - *oh mother, oh father - dear departed, let the moon show his evil face.* And nobody giving a shell (a derogatory term arrived at from the shell-like motif on the old Upper currency).'

It was true that we knew the mechanisms of the disease. But not the reality. Not most of us. Or we knew partial things. There were things Zee was unaware of. She did not know the function of the White Rooms. I was sure she had never seen any white-bodying - though I never asked her. It was a different world, subearth, to an Upper. But we didn't question that reality. The subs lived in disease. We could not risk integrating them. And they had been our enemies in the past. We allowed them to come as helpers; wasn't that something? We hadn't necessarily to take the risk. And they had to remember that it was Upper scientists that had invented the shot. We didn't exclude subs from buying shots. There were subs I had on record who had bought the serum. But I couldn't say these things to her. We even suppressed many diseases with vaccinations in the food we sold them. They laid all the blame on us. But it wasn't the whole story.

The mother came back into the room. She came as silence took over, except for the drumming of the rain, and I wondered if she had been listening to our conversation. The room we were in was small and cluttered but the mother and daughter moved with greater freedom than I or my wife did in our own home. The fate of Zee's father was never mentioned.

The mother smiled at me and turned to Zee and nodded.

'It's time,' the girl said.

I looked at them both. Zee leant forward and placed a hand on my leg. A shudder spiralled down my spine. I felt enclosed, cocooned and yet imprisoned at the same time. In a strange way I was also in the "oubliette".

I followed them through to a hallway. Only the candle the mother carried and a candle in the hallway gave light. The smell of the wax was rich. Stairs were revealed when heavy curtains were parted. We climbed. At the top of the stairs was a small landing with three doors leading off. The candlelight was caught by a draft and shifted the shadows. The bizarre situation I had contrived to get myself in was almost humorous, I thought flippantly. Except that what I was proposing to do was highly illegal – deadly serious.

We looked into the room. The mother lifted the candle high. I saw the child asleep. He was beautiful - as his mother. Seeing him there made the danger concrete. I was in charge of Records for my region. If I had caught an Upper doing what I was doing it would have meant a permanent stay in subearth - without shots. Zee and one of my colleagues had transgressed the laws. It was these laws I had stood resolutely by since becoming a man. You couldn't count share-shuffling... One of my colleagues had effectively put our world at risk. If the disease mutated through an off-spring then - shot or no shot -

we could all have ended as subs. But this man did it for Zee. For lust. And even as I think now, I remember how she looked then. And I wanted her too. But all of those thoughts on my first visit to subearth are long gone.

Staring at the child reinforced my fear for my as yet, unborn baby. Of course I would help them. They knew that I wouldn't be able to dissociate this innocence and beauty with the child growing in my wife's womb. Besides they also knew that exposing relations between a work colleague (one I had chosen) and one of my helpers would not be a good career move. Already it was too late. I was trapped. Trapped in a cell without windows. Upwards (through a mystical shaft) lay salvation.

The child slept as I thought.

'You see?' Zee said to me, standing close by.

I nodded.

'You'll take him?' asked the mother.

I peered down into his cot. He was about six months old. It could be arranged. I had the ability to transfer papers. Many children were still-born in our world. There mightn't even be the need for the orphanage (where only the mentally-handicapped babies remained - nicknamed "subs", not sent to the White Rooms and who knows - I thought with new cynicism – perhaps kept for transplants too). There would be people willing to take him on as their own. I could do that anonymously, I considered. Then I checked myself. What was I getting out of all this?

'Will you do it?' Zee asked. Did she read my mind? Did she notice the changing expressions on my face? The mother left the room and with us and the child in darkness. Zee came to me and lifting herself kissed the side of my mouth. Was this my reward? I thought of my wife and the child growing in her and I smelt the scent of the beautiful young woman. Another reckless act offered itself up to me. I couldn't resist embracing her. But you have to know - I didn't break the rules. Not the government Record rules anyway.

With my eyes staring at the ceiling, my body felt lifeless. Her smooth and naked body lay next to mine, one of her hands resting awkwardly on my side. I hadn't broken the rules (quite) but I felt like a dog. I would have to tell my wife I had worked even longer hours at the office. Thank god for the secrecy. Thank god for the Record and Registry office.

A snuffle escaped the baby's mouth. The room was pitch-black. With all my soul I wanted to do the ancient thing with her. Rain splashed against a hidden window pain. Before light we would have to begin the journey back. I would become a "father" before my time.

In her sleep she was restless. Foreshadowing the action of my wife Jo, Zee forced me to hunt for spiders before she would finally sleep. Perhaps that was the final bizarre act. As a helper she should have been able to sniff the things out of dark corners. But her fear of spiders was real enough. For all I knew, and was insanely dismissive of, there might have been a spider crawling up through the waste pipes at that very moment. But I'm jumping the gun of my story. Later I was to be infected - back then I was clean. And regular shots (usually) kept me that way, and kept me a chasm's distance from all the subs. Even the beautiful sub that lay next to me in the bed.

Chapter 4

It still seemed like the middle of the night when we awoke. Even in the early hours Zee looked serenely beautiful. She kissed me. I wasn't sure why. As she got out of bed I saw the gracefulness of her limbs. And the startling purity of her flesh in the ray of moonlight creeping in. The rain had stopped and the air smelt damp. She picked up her child. Her belly was flat – showed no sign of its pre-birth heaviness. She was strong and fit – had to be. I got up too and instinctively went to draw the curtain.

'No,' she barked. The curtains were thin and the moon was full but disappearing behind the rooftops. The sky was mercifully clear of smoke.

With automatic assumptions she handed me the baby and lit a candle. The whole atmosphere of the place was changed. Again shadows closed us in. The boy wriggled sleepily against my chest. I had never held a baby before then. She gave me a measured look. Briefly she spied through a hole in the curtain cloth and mouthed, 'Bloody cat,' before turning to me. Holding out her hands she expected an automatic response. There was complete quiet as I gave her the soft flesh. Then a scream erupted from outside.

'Nothing,' she said. 'Just some crazy sub unusually close, perhaps.'

We went downstairs silently.

I was left in the front room as she went back upstairs with the child to see her mother. There was muffled crying and words I couldn't make out. Sipping the weak, warm grog, I thought of the excuses I would give to Jo. And I began to wonder about the practical looking-after of the baby boy until I could get him legal papers. And I was also aware of a tremendous flow of blood through my system. I was exhilarated. There was an inward smile at my rebellious act. It was real. What I was doing was real. And meaningful - I quickly told myself.

Zee came down with tears in her eyes. 'I have to feed,' she said.

And again, for the first time, I realised that for her this was no game. That she was giving up her child for a better life. It was a cold slap of realism - no game at all. I sat watching her feed the baby in a kind of mystical silence. Occasionally she paid me attention. Or she told me where things were and what to pack in the bags. Finally she told me to take something from a drawer in the chest squeezed into the cluttered small room. I pulled out a toy.

'I want him to keep this,' she said pulling the baby's wet mouth from her teat. The boy gurgled. He had not cried. It was as if he were stupefied and now nourished and content.

'I'll try and get work as a helper in the household,' she said suddenly, 'but I'll need your help.' I took her words for granted. It seemed the government official was no more than a puppet. Perhaps no more than a helpless baby.

'Yes,' I replied tamely.

'Time to go,' she said.

We were about to leave when I heard the buzzing of an insect and saw a wasp in a jar. She must have noticed my reaction. 'It protects,' she tried to explain.

'Against what?'

'Against the spiders of course,' and it seemed she spat the word out. 'Wasps kill them,' she explained further. 'Wasps, mice and rats.'

'Is it true?' I asked.

'Don't you know anything?'

I met her gaze and kept it.

'That's why we hate cats so much. Cats kill the rodents.'

'But cats kill birds too, and birds must surely eat wasps.'

'Have you seen any birds?' she asked scornfully.

And it was true that I had not.

In defiance I thought, she unscrewed the jar and released the wasp as we left the tiny house. All I could think to say, as I held the baby for her, was, 'But they sting.' She simply laughed. Taking the baby back she urged me to check the bags were safe. 'Come on,' she said. I followed her. Earlier that night, that day, we had been almost as lovers. Zee demanded a high price.

Before we left the town in subearth (I later discovered it was called Wayland), she said she wanted to show me something else.

'Isn't that too dangerous?' I asked, wary of time passing.

'It's okay, the sun is a few hours away. Only the mad ones are about. We have time.'

'But think of the baby.'

'I am,' cutting me short.

The boy was falling asleep again. I was grateful for his easy temperament. My stomach rumbled with hunger pangs.

'It's on the way,' she said as consolation.

There were still subs awake in the dirty corners of shaky houses and empty shops. We passed a brazier burning bright, sending up ashes and with stiff bodies crushed next to it, keeping warm. Turning down a urine smelling alleyway we seemed to enter a ruined part of the town. She stepped over some cobbled stones holding the baby carefully. Time to time he would let out a kind of panicked squeak and then, almost incredibly, revert to sleep.

'In here,' she said. I followed warily. 'Look through here.' I went to the barred window. The glass was semi-opaque but I could see inside. There were shapes of monkeys and muffled screams. 'What is it? What are they?'

'Chimpanzees,' she said flatly, 'tested on for the disease. They were the first ones used - before the last war. We've inherited them from your scientists. Sometimes they escape and the disease mutates. They've raped women; killed men. There are wild colonies across su - and a pack which freely roams about this town.'

'Why don't you kill them?' I asked rationally.

'What with?'

'You have guns.'

She laughed. 'Not any more. More of your fiction. The only guns are way, way south of here (as I would find out much later). Close to the mystery lands,' she said enigmatically. 'Even if we get a gun and ammunition we can't outrun them. The healthy ones won't risk it. These chimps have the disease but it affects them differently. That's why your Upper scientists got it so wrong,' she smiled. 'But sometimes a chimp is cornered and the brave left amongst us capture it. Sometimes.'

'Why are you showing me? Why are you telling me all this?'

'Because none of you want to know. You take limbs from us, you watch us fight - you know, come on. You wage war if we dare to speak out. And you left us with these hairy ones who rampage. Next time you see a crazed sub watch out for the bite marks or the torn flesh. A zombie isn't quick on its feet. And now you know something of this hell I know you will do anything to protect my boy.'

'Why just him?' I began to argue.

She laughed. 'Let's carry on,' she said, 'we're too close for comfort.'

'See, you're risking his life,' I said in a hurt tone.

'I'm saving his life.'

'But those...those *things*...'

'I have this,' she said suddenly and took a pistol from her trouser back pocket.

'How?'

'I'm a helper,' she smiled. Changing the timbre of her voice she added, 'You're a good man. I know that. We know that. You're just obeying orders I know. Only kidding. But down here you'd be lost. For all you have in your world - down here you couldn't survive. Not without fire (the term used for weaponry).'

The buildings began to thin out and on the close horizon I could make out the huts where the "lucky" diseased subs ended their days. At different points on the outskirts of the town there would either be one main hut or a cluster of smaller huts. We sat behind a wall and rested. There had been a change in the light. Zee's eyes scanned the ground around her. 'Spiders,' she said.

'I'm kind of surprised there are any left.'

'These bastards reproduce constantly. We kill them and more appear. Okay, in houses it's unusual now. The disease gets spread by body fluids. You could be unlucky enough to be sneezed on...with your mouth open,' she added. I detected a kind of bravado as she spoke. This was where she was from and her people knew how to cope. It was me and my type who were the weak ones.

'We kill them, the wasps and mice kill them...'

'But the mice and rats bring disease...'

'A nothing disease,' she stated. 'You know for a long time we didn't even know it was the spiders. Now it's almost always the humans - but the fear spreads. And you (she always addressed me as some kind of ambassador of the Uppers), you could have killed them all if you had wanted to. You had the chemicals, the poisons to do that.'

'No that isn't true,' I argued, and I knew something about that. 'When we tried to kill the spiders there was nothing that didn't affect us too. We aren't immune from the fear...'

'Just the disease,' she added.

'Yes,' I conceded.

'Then why not give this immunity to us, eh?'

'There isn't enough serum. You have no idea how much it costs to produce. Don't you think we'd give it to everyone if we could? It would be in our own interest.'

Her look told me that she didn't believe me. The baby opened his eyes and began to cry. Taking him she rocked him in her arms. Their world was brutal. At that moment I was glad to have been born an Upper.

We left the town before the stump-limbed bodies roused themselves. I thought with sleep they might experience dreams where they could once again run and breathe freely. But those out of their minds never slept, it seemed. Right until the earth road leading to the start of the rough tarmac highway the crazy ones came.

'Where's youse a goin' with little-un eh?' We ignored. 'Tell yer old mammy now. Tell yer muffer.' Zee looked at me - eyes telling me to leave conversation out. 'Won't yer tell us now?'

'Theyse from the other-world, ain't they? You from the bridge, mister? You got the look. You got the face, pretty boy,' said another.

'What's the bridge?' I asked Zee later.

'It's kind of a heaven to them. Somehow they share this illusion. That there's a bridge that will take them away from subearth.'

'Why not?' I said.

'Because it doesn't exist,' she answered coldly.

'You're going to have to keep him quiet, you understand?' I said. 'The guards aren't going to turn a blind eye to a baby.'

'Sure.'

'You're going to have to hide him somehow.'

'I've thought all about that *Mr Adam, sir,*' her tone changed.

She changed clothes. She dressed the way a helper would. I liked the shortness of her dress but she quickly put on a long coat. The sun was spreading its light across the horizon but there was a chill wind.

'I'm giving him grog,' she said.

'Will that be okay?'

'It made you warm right enough?'

'Yes.'

'It'll send the poor soul to sleep,' she said with hidden warmth. 'I'll wrap him up and put him in a basket in the back. We'll hear nothing from him. They won't search us, will they?'

'No,' I replied.

As the border approached we said nothing to each other. I could feel fear from her. And for the first time as an Upper I sensed something terrible hanging over me. Some sense of the transience of life and the hell that might await us. The guards knew I was in authority. Besides, the car meant I had money - and money and authority were synonymous.

'Your papers,' said the guard. Zee observed me. They had not asked on the way in, but sometimes there were scares or pretended scares. It was all done for morale. I handed the young guard my papers. 'And the girl,' he ordered politely. It was strange. As an official in Records I didn't expect such treatment.

'Is anything wrong?' I asked neutrally.

'No sir.'

'It's not usual for me,' I said. I didn't want to appear apprehensive. Though I had never been out of the country before I had had to show papers at the borders of factories and research units in Upper. I had had to show papers when rising through the ranks also – to those who mattered.

'The girl's,' the guard repeated patiently.

I handed him Zee's. 'She's a helper,' I explained. The guard half smiled.

The guard went into the office. We were left waiting. 'Is everything all right?' Zee whispered.

'Sshh.'

The young guard reappeared with an older officer. They looked at us and then looked at the back of the car. Sweat formed in my palm which, unconsciously, I was pressing my fingernails into. As they turned we heard the slightest sound from the baby. Checking my rear-view mirror I saw the younger guard sweep his head round. Then he walked to my side of the car.

'Everything okay?' I asked.

For a long moment his eyes darted between the both of us. 'Quite all right,' he said at last. 'There has been some trouble with bandits,' he explained. 'We have to tighten up, sir.'

I straightened, 'Of course.'

'Go ahead,' the guard said.

We moved off. But just as we reached the second barrier it closed in front of us. 'They know,' said Zee, 'drive on, drive through, make a run for it.'

'No,' I said turning to her. The older officer came up to the car.

'Excuse me,' he said as I lowered the window. Condensation had steamed the glass. The officer was well wrapped up but still cold.

'Yes officer?'

'I'm sorry,' he said, 'but it is our custom,' he fished in his pocket, 'would you like to give to our charity. We have many problems working out here. Wives and children to support. Please, if you can, give generously.'

I looked carefully into his steely-grey eyes. Then I felt inside my jacket pocket. Taking out a thousand I handed it over.

'Thank you sir,' he smiled, 'I'm sorry to have detained you or delayed you. Have a good journey.'

As we pulled under the raised barrier I said 'Bastards' under my breath. Then the baby cried. Zee laughed forcibly. 'I'll give the wee one some more grog,' she said.

'Yes,' I said.

The horizon was getting lighter. Colours were spreading in layers. Jo would still be asleep. It seemed like another lifetime in the Upper world. And it seemed another existence in the world where I had slept close to Zee.

'I'll drop you off in the office,' I said, 'you'll be safe there. I can lock you in with a security key. You might have to stay until the afternoon. I'll have to smooth things with Jo first. Then we'll get the baby looked after.' And then it occurred to me that I didn't even know the small thing's name. 'What is he called?' I asked at last.

Smiling, she answered, 'Adam.' She was clever.

'Of course,' I replied.

The car sped up and lifted from the tarmac - free and fast.

Chapter 5

Lying next to Jo I let thoughts race through my mind. Nightmares haunted my every sleep. Jo was breathing heavily. Comfortable. There had been no spiders to trouble her – since the night of the party she had asked me to check our room before she could fall safely asleep. I rubbed my big toe against the softie – nothing. I lay back on the bed and could have cried. Two worlds had converged - equally surreal; the world below – "su" - and the dawning of some terrible new-world in Upper – and that these worlds converged, collided, because of me.

How long would it take for the disease to spread? Was my old-world about to collapse? I tried to wake earlier in the morning and go to bed later than Jo. But I was as kind as I could be. The slice into my big toe would never heal but I could, at least, conceal it. But I resolved to see a doctor I knew who was bent enough to keep things quiet. I knew him because I once did him a favour. That was all I needed – the doctor and some credit. Maybe I could sort things out.

About seven years previously I had been sent to investigate a case of rule-breaching. In those days I worked many hours away from the office. It was just before Jo and I had got married. A doctor had been accused of sexual relations with a young helper girl. In fact it was a trumped-up charge by a disgruntled patient. This patient had had a crush on the doctor and when he did not return her advances (which would have contravened article 214) she turned spiteful. At first she used only to constantly book appointments at the clinic, but then she complained about her treatment. She would also bad-mouth the doctor to all who took the time to listen, further alienating the doctor who, naturally, refused to see her as his patient. This only exacerbated her response.

Eventually the woman went a step too far and approached the helpers in his household (apparently this was with the idea of getting access to his private life), she noticed that one of the helpers - a young girl - was very pretty and hit on the idea of accusing the doctor of gross misconduct. Not only medical misconduct, of course. And that was why I had been brought in. But as the investigation proceeded it became obvious what had gone on. The woman herself got into trouble. The doctor had to move practices. But during the searches (routine procedure) I came upon material that would have damaged the doctor's career for good. Would have put him behind closed doors.

Locked away, perhaps even forgotten, I found printed material (itself an indication of a rebellious mind) containing graphic accounts and pictures of illegal limb transplants (so you see I *knew*). Explicit pictures of dismembered but still living subs and gratefully posed Uppers waving proud new arms and legs. (But I would never have admitted this to Zee. Perhaps I couldn't really admit it to myself – perhaps I thought that this kind of practice was long since dead. In Upper there was selective amnesia. Officially and un-officially sanctioned amnesia.) There were also shots of grafted sexual genitalia. Much of the work dealt with routine transplanting of internal organs. But at the end of the bound papers there was a picture of a full head transplant. The operation for so doing rambled on for about ten thousand words - many of which I could not comprehend.

But I didn't shop the doctor. I didn't shop him because that wasn't what I was investigating and also because I liked him. And it gave me a thrill to think people would still risk everything by "discovering" such stuff. Maybe I didn't want to become involved in the tedious amount of tap-work (computer input) that would have been involved so close to the wedding. At first I considered that perhaps Jo's father might change his opinion of me for the better, but then I thought otherwise. I didn't want any disruptions to a wedding that was already being seen as one big mighty disruption. The simple fact was that there existed a kind of official schizophrenia. We knew and we didn't know. I knew things and yet, honestly, I disbelieved them simultaneously.

The doctor was grateful. We kept in touch for a while. He was eventually struck off from practising for breaking a minor relationship-rule. I read the dossier on that case. The doctor had inappropriately touched a young girl (thirteen years old). She was an

Upper so he didn't get placed on the Register. I pictured him working at the edges of our world. Wondered if he put into practice any of the bizarre things he had been studying. Before we lost contact he had said that he was doing research into all kinds of things - exciting things. I didn't ask too much; you could never trust the 'phones. You can never trust the 'phones – not even ear transplants.

Later at work sitting down in my office, I blanked the screen of the 'phone and talked to the doctor again. This was risky – but worth it. Casting my eyes around the room I recalled how Zee and the child had been brought here before I fixed the papers. After the nervousness at the border everything had gone smoothly enough. I thought how it was Zee who had got me into the mess I was in right then. Mess? I trivialised my position. Unconsciously I stubbed my unfeeling toe. I had the beginning of the disease – there was *nothing* in the world worse than that.

After we got out of subearth I took Zee to the Government buildings with the child. Nobody thought anything unusual about that. Though dawn had recently broken, and the beginnings of the hiss had started (the hiss is the name we give to urban traffic), my behaviour was un-noteworthy. Sometimes I questioned helpers in my office. Sometimes the children who were brought in were never seen again. The security staff was trained not to see the obvious.

In the room used for interrogation I left her with baby Adam. 'You'll be all right,' I had said, 'nobody will disturb you.'

'How long will you be?'

'I don't know. There's food and drink here,' I opened a cabinet. 'Take it easy, don't worry, the worst is over. I'll make enquiries this afternoon. The baby will be fine.' As I left I suddenly had violent feelings towards my secret colleague who had caused such distress. A baby would have to be separated from its mother because of his selfish lust.

Arriving home I took the lift straight to our apartment and let myself in. Jo was still in bed. The time was nine-thirty. Yet time had speeded up. And in a curious way slowed down enough to allow so much to happen. I was dead-beat. I slunked down in a guest room and fell asleep. Dreams of grotesque figures filled my mind.

Jo arose late - thank god. Innocent that she was she thought nothing had happened but a long night's work. The kind soul (mellowed by an early sense of "motherhood") came in and draped an extra softie over me. It was late when I finally came round, exhausted, famished and thirsty.

I didn't feel proud of myself; for lying in words and lying, physically with Zee. But already I felt different. There was a kind of elation that went with the deception and a kind of justification. The truth was I had set myself outside of the laws - the laws that I helped lay down. And for why? For a beautiful face? For a reckless moment? For compassion? Nothing I thought explained the nature of my transgression. Only the fact was left.

Once I had taken the decision to step outside the norm things ran smoothly. I was affectionate with my wife. I drove steadily to work (late afternoon); found papers that were easily doctored and a family that could take the child and cover-up their past effectively. Anything that might have gone wrong would have meant instant execution - I suppose. Better that.

Zee told me she was due back on duty the following day (I didn't know). There was a tearful parting from Adam that I could barely witness. The new mother was grateful and cold. Her son had died three years previously and her most recent pregnancy terminated after four months (like so many). All she had to do was conceal the child and "disappear" for a while. I had the means to write out papers that would allow her free travel. Many women "disappeared" and returned with children; or with new personalities; or new lives. It was the way of our world. Sanatoriums littered the southern coast and potent men pimped themselves freely. (We needed children. And so you might wonder that a society in need of children would so mercilessly kill them. But we did. And do, I presume. That is why we have the White Rooms.)

The child whose name was coded as Adam **** was registered as having been born at **** on **** to the woman and her husband. They had money, and enough grief to risk anything. Zee watched her son leave in the arms of this woman. The baby was quiet and beautiful. The woman and baby were given covering documents. I had to tap in some extra notes into the records afterwards. Much of my work was re-writing history. A kind of multitudinous personal history. When I came back Zee had disappeared. *And that was only the beginning of my troubles.*

It was only a few days later that I received the first note - coded of course. The note was short and to the point. They wanted money. I could have laughed when I read it. The whole world sank to my bowels and I truly did nearly laugh. Then I vomited into the toilet basin. Later, sitting in my favourite chair I quietly seethed with anger. They were blackmailing me for saving their son. A boy who might have grown up in a dirty, disease ridden town. A boy whose brain could have been eaten from the inside as his limbs were numbed from the outside. A smile like a wound gashed my face. The irony was not lost.

All that is history. But they had brought me to where I was then. So I made contact with the doctor. How else was I to get a cheap shot and the chance to fight the numbness? That dag numbness that constantly ate up my thoughts – so that my mind was left numb. At least my mind was not being eaten by the disease. Dag forbid.

The blackmail had arrived electronically. Either I owned up to my transgression or I paid up. No choice. Of course I tried to find out who it was but my surreptitious appeals for help didn't work. I was stuck with the demands - and the demands I paid. The blackmailer knew exactly how I was to pay the credits without involving the system. I suppose I was chosen because of my security clearance. It all made me feel ill and foolish. But I coped.

The first thing I determined was to track down the girl. But she had quickly left my employ and was no longer in our world it seemed. Quite legitimately she could have crossed the border back to subearth or was holing up illegally. My hands were tied. I could not use the baby to stop them as everything connected me. Neat. But I wasn't at all sure why they were blackmailing me. That part was naive I suppose. But I was to discover a complexity beyond my narrow rationale.

Once I paid the credits there was no stopping "him". I got drained. All the while my child was growing in the womb and my wife becoming more adorable. Except I was getting cold and distant. And irritable. And yet I tried to keep everything together. At work I was suspicious of everyone. Paranoia was soaking my spirit. And the blackmailer was soaking my reserves. Just when things appeared they could get no worse, some shares I had shuffled, before the nightmare, bombed. And even that was not quite that.

My shot was due. My shot was due and I could not afford it. No matter what I thought up I could not raise the money. There was nothing Jo would fall for. And Jo's father had been my only hope. But I convinced myself that I could do without the shot. Explaining to my (legitimate) doctor that I was going elsewhere for the jab I lost a good ally. Again I was able to re-write my personal history. By that stage I didn't much care. The whole of the Upper world was re-writing and programming history. And I was a fool – a hanged man.

If there was anything to say in my defence it was that I did call in enough favours to ensure my wife's shot could be paid for. In that way I was protecting her and the baby from the possibility of the disease and also disgrace. To be associated with a loser would have damaged her. But she had much worse to come.

That was the position I was in so recently. And then it got worse. Having a shot is a big deal and big expense. I was never one to maintain payment plans (not even Jo's – though she never went without shots) or take out or afford insurance; I had never before been blackmailed. And that dirty bastard arachnid must have known the squeeze on me. Must have watched me suffer. And known that his child lived and had shots because I stuck out my neck. And knew that my family was in big danger.

In the end there was nothing I could do but go in search of Zee. If I found her I knew at least that I could get to the blackmailer. Simple. The difficult part was taking time from work and convincing my wife that I had to go away on business. She didn't fall for it - but she was fuller in the belly. And she had to live the lie. All she begged was to know who the woman was. I think I convinced her eventually there was no other. But I must have scared her half to death with what I only half said.

Joining the hiss of the world I flowed straight then turned for the border. This time I knew what to expect. This time I had no shot in my body. But I was still brave then. Still thinking I was immortal. Still thinking I was wronged. That I was a good man. Still independent of bent doctors. And though I could not know for sure I was somehow confident that Zee would be back in the tiny rat-infested house in Wayland.

The border crossing approached. I was still a free man and a man of rank. A healthy man. A disease-free man. Life hung on. Just.

Chapter 6

Going back is always difficult. Going back into subearth territory was like revisiting a nightmare. I had had no problem crossing the border and was soon exchanging neat metal-way for primitive earth and stone roads - tyres touching or skimming lightly. Remembering where to halt, I camouflaged the car and got dressed in shabby clothes.

It was terrifying to be alone in that place. For one, I did not know how exactly to find Zee's house. None of my other helpers opened up or confessed in response to my oblique questions. There was only the map in my mind and the incidents I had experienced that I hoped would help me recall the way. I should have used my digital – but I didn't want to leave any trace.

Finding the outskirts of town was easy enough but I missed the huts. At first I didn't recognise anything. Trying to blend into the background I kept my eyes to the ground. Subs watched me. There seemed to be a conspiracy in their collective deformity. But they had only grown deformed through the bluntness of life. Limbs had been rubbed away. Even when I could smell their decaying bodies and glanced quickly into their narrow white eyes, I never lost sympathy.

Though it was daylight, fires still burned. There were hardly more people about than at night. More children scuttled between the adult subs' stumbling, clumsy legs and there seemed more body-dealers (usually painted-up girls and women). I began to notice the cats strung up on poles and the rats led by strings and leather leads (at least these rats wouldn't bite the flesh of dying subs). There were many insects in the air also. Shops were open. Casually I looked inside some of these - nothing appeared fresh or plentiful.

As the centre neared and the streets closed in I lost my way. The subs seemed to know I was not one of them for they eyed me curiously. With their contracted pupils they appeared malevolent. If they had found out I was a lone Upper they would probably have torn me apart.

My pace quickened with growing anxiety. Each turn I made must have taken me farther from the right route. I grew sick looking at the hobbling bodies, the scalded flesh and the gaping blood-less wounds. The subs were in the constant process of *slowing*. They were all heading for the stillness of eternity. If they were "perfect" this would probably be by way of the long-huts. And the others? I presumed they would be burnt on pyres if not eaten by rats.

Eventually I turned into a crumbling part of the town and was shocked to a standstill. I was not entirely lost. Without realising it I had found my way to the area where Zee had shown me the chimpanzees. And as if on cue I saw a sub with teeth marks that had serrated the edge of her skin - a clump of missing flesh torn away. Had a chimpanzee bitten the flesh from her? Had she struggled; felt pain? Were her limbs numb to the savage biting? I hoped so. And I pictured her defenceless, hobbling from the muscular grip of the animal. Was it content with its chalky flesh - was it content to let her go? Or did she fight it off somehow? Or did other subs feel the need to come to her rescue?

Watching her stumble and pick up her dead legs just enough to hobble onwards I realised what easy pickings the subs were. And yet there were others who had not contracted the disease. And I wondered if these were the ones from whom the shots had been developed by my own government's scientists. As far as I knew the ingredients used for the shots were grown in government controlled labs - but it occurred to me for the first time how really - and perhaps artificially - expensive shots were (though I had little idea what they consisted of). It occurred to me then because I thought there might be an easier way to get some shots. And maybe a way to shoot them up everyone; sub and Upper alike. It occurred to me then too because I was unprotected.

In a short time I had thought thoughts that were alien to the likes of me. There was no reason to think in the side (laterally); we were trained not to. There was no need. Things worked and worked well - unless you transgressed. Unless you had relations with a sub - or you got taken in by a beautiful sub-girl. I suddenly thought about the baby, Adam, and my own child growing inside its mother. Up to that point I had never felt lonelier or more lost.

And then I saw a sight that quite unnerved me - and sent my expectations of that world tumbling. A procession of subs turned a corner of the crumbling, rubble-strewn terrace of houses. In the midst of this procession was held aloft a chimpanzee tied by its front and back limbs to a metal pole. It was quite alive and struggled desperately and continuously. From time to time a gaggle of little able-bodied children poked darts into its fur – two other children hobbling behind. With amazement I watched the subs march past. And I followed as the primate burst into deafening screams.

It might have been crazy to follow but I was drawn somehow. Before too long the subs reached a clearing. Appearing like a bomb crater, a hollow surrounded by houses opened up and revealed a huge fire burning at its centre. The procession moved down the hollow and spread about the fire. The chimp - or more accurately the pole holding the chimp - was balanced between two supporting collections of stakes. Beneath its now struggle-free swing (had it resigned itself to a terrible fate?) there were the logs and kindling of a prepared fire. Next to it and sending hot burning ashes into the air the huge fire roared.

A boy approached me. I must have been hanging back suspiciously.

'Grunne bin gret eh?'

Thinking quickly I answered, 'Aye, tis right.' It seemed to satisfy him. All eyes were on the limply hanging body. Then a quite sprightly sub came forwards (was he one of those who had actually captured the animal?) and placed a torch of flame into the wood. Fire rose fast. There was a hush from those gathered and the chimp expelled an excruciating cry. The sound rented the air. The sound shot down my spine. I realised I was not one of those people - that something deeper divided us. I turned my gaze from the screaming animal but the smell of its singed fur clogged my nose. I realised again that this was not a game I was playing. Reckless as I might be I was not share-shuffling. Oh how I longed for the security of my wife and home. Cursing Zee under my breath and the curves of her body, I slipped away. At least, I figured, the chimpanzees would be far away.

The roads and streets were depressingly similar in their appearance. Shabby doorway upon doorway confused me. But I was sure once I saw the house of Zee's other life I would recognise it. In retrospect I was extremely naive - but as is often the way this very naiveté led me to a street I recalled from the dark night of my previous visit. Walking up and down I looked for clues. Still I couldn't decide if it was the correct place. Did I need to turn down a back lane? I also knew that I wasn't to attract attention to myself. Already upstairs curtains were twitching and the children who were playing (including some with the disease) had begun to take notice of me.

As I neared a damp smelling alleyway I heard a voice calling. First looking around I nipped into the arched passageway and held my breath. It was then that I realised this was the way I had taken with Zee. The call came again, its direction from the back of one of the houses. A sub stumbled out of a connecting pathway and I saw stump-like fingers on his hands. It was important for me not to gaze. There was nothing friendly passed between us. I held my breath. This was the closest I had come to the disease. Before I had been protected - even when I had fought off a sub with his knife – but on that second visit I was dangerously at risk. The disease past me by in the shape of the sub and I could only imagine the extent of his suffering.

The door I was leaning on gave way. A hand pulled me through. It was Zee's mother. The diseased sub lurched from wall to wall. Already his mind was decomposing; shutting out the connections which kept us sane and human. I had seen the eyes of some of the subs dulled by grog or by creeping insanity. I could still feel the air which had past between me and the diseased body. The touch of Zee's mother alarmed me.

'Come,' she said, 'be gettin' yer in. Okay?'

Inside the house a wasp buzzed wearily. I began to notice more things. The mother sat me down and made me a grog. The place smelt of unwholesome food and was generally damp. It was then I noticed how everything was sealed up. Stoppers on the bottom of the doors and the windows shut tight. I let myself be taken over by the mother's almost indifferent hospitality. She was scared - somewhere deep, deep down. There appeared to be no police in subearth (and yet in our world we had heard so many stories of paramilitary brutality), perhaps, I thought, justice was meted out by the mob - as was the case with the chimpanzee.

'There,' she said, giving me the drink. I felt awkward being there, imposing myself. I did not know what she knew about me.

'Thank you,' I said meekly.

'Youse found yourself back then?' Her manner of speaking seemed more mannered than the others I had heard in subearth but not as cultured as her daughter or any other helper.

'I have to see her,' I said.

'She's not here.'

'Where is she?'

'What youse want to see her for?'

I knew by the way the mother said this that she had been told about me. Zee had confided in her. 'I need her help,' I said honestly.

'Help what for?'

'I need to...Look, I'm in trouble. I haven't...' and I mimicked a needle going into my arm. She didn't seem to comprehend. 'A shot,' I explained. The mother nodded her head. 'Takin' a chance then, youse be.'

'I have no choice,' I said firmly. 'Now, do you know where she is?'

'She's been let down,' the mother said furtively.

We spoke some more about nothing. What was I to say to that woman? I was an Upper. Her daughter had been my helper. Her daughter had transgressed and it seemed been double-crossed, perhaps, by her lover. The woman told me of the ills and deaths that had befallen her family and how they - as "clean" ones - were often spat at or worse in the street. Credit (she used "money") came through a son who worked in the fields – and from Zee. The whole economy of subearth relied on handouts from the Upper world. And again it dawned on me just how little I knew and how little cross talk there appeared to be between government departments. And was I such a prominent figure as I thought in that government? She eventually asked me about Adam – I could feel her apprehension. But I was able to put her at ease. He was – after all – safe.

After taking more grog and eating a pitiful stew I rested in the room where I had slept with Zee and baby Adam. The air was stale and lifeless. My metabolism seemed to slow. The mother had told me she would search for her daughter. I assumed she knew exactly where Zee was. I wondered about Zee's plans to be a helper in Adam's new "family". But she was too smart to get caught out so soon. I could easily have found her. I had checked.

Eventually I fell asleep and into a bizarre landscape of disturbed dreams. Rivers cut swathes through loose soil. Then, as they swirled in malevolent currents, I waded across. Volcanoes sent up fountains of black liquid and the earth dragged me down. Towns and cities out of a childhood interaction game suddenly appeared upon a flat desert land. No water. Just black monolithic buildings. Then that dream cut to me held inside a cellar. No windows and no light. A huge wasp flew through the dank air. And then an extremely beautiful butterfly - quite out of keeping with the monochrome dream - landed on my face. But I felt some kind of needle-prick into the side wall of my nose.

At that point it was almost as if I awoke out of my dream. Before me stood Zee. I remember that her face and body were blurred. But I could not say if I were dreaming or otherwise. Then the mother appeared and they talked in whispers and seemed to care for me.

I still remember Zee's words. She said:

Adam, I am waiting for him to come to me. I didn't want things to go the way they did - believe me. He went too far. Don't think badly of me or him. We needed the money. There is a land, far away, remember...the mystery land. He will get me a shot and take the baby from your world. Then we will leave here. But he went too far. He should never have bled you the way he did. He doesn't understand the danger. Like you. He doesn't understand. Forgive me.

In the midst of my nightmares her voice came as clear as a mountain stream.

When I came to from my sleep I realised how I ached all over and that sweat had poured from me. Zee had disappeared. I rubbed the side of my nose. Couldn't feel anything. The mother gave me grog. I asked her the time. I remember that it was night.

I said, 'Have I slept long?'

She smiled. 'Yes.'

'I must see your daughter.'

Smiling again the mother said, 'She has spoken with you. You have been ill. Youse have lain here for two days.'

'Two days?'

The woman nodded.

'It can't be.'

'It is so.'

'Ill?' I asked.

Zee's mother looked kindly at me – said nothing.

'I must return,' I said and forced myself onto my elbows. 'What has been wrong with me?'

Now that I recall all that transpired, I realise why the mother of Zee cast her eyes to the ground and lied to me. For the day previous to the two sweat-ridden nights, I had been bitten by a spider. Must have been. It was a fluke. A low chance. It still happened. It happened to me. It happened in a disease-free house, with the air locked-in tight and with wasps buzzing in cracks and crevices. But back then I didn't know the truth and I wouldn't have wanted to have known. Just as I fought the truth as my toe began to go numb at the dinner party much later.

The way out of su was as nauseating as the way in - but I had the true look of the disease to their practised eyes.

Back in my own world things erupted between Jo and I. Then we made up and I began to live a lie. And still the blackmail came. Credits were directed straight from my source. Less than before and I thanked god. Dinner parties and Jo's growing stomach veiled the reality of what was happening. Until the numbness came. And then it was shortly after that I remembered the doctor. *The doctor who was my only hope.*

My marriage was fragile. I had no credit. I had the symptoms of the disease. If the disease was what my worst fears imagined, only the bent doctor could save me from a descent into the underworld - the slow deterioration of the body and mind. And then perhaps I would pray for the mind to be lost quickly. But I recalled the long-huts with the subs laid out and their staring eyes.

The mighty Exmass was approaching. The time of the holy-fuck. My child would be born soon after. Before Zee approached me I was a good man with a good job. I vomited with the thought. I could no longer eat. But I kept up appearances. Kept throwing parties. Because I knew one of the bastards that I invited was the man who had brought me so low. And I would get hold of Zee once the doctor had done his business. The doctor was my only hope. My only god-worship, holy-fuck hope.

Chapter 7

The doctor lived in one of the slummier parts of the Upper world. A place where gleaming chrome and sun-spangled glass gave way to dull metal and wood. But it was still superior in every way to subearth – it had all the basic amenities. He had made a tenuous living serving the baser needs of the Uppers. When we had corresponded I asked him details of his life. I was, after all, the government official and still had power over him. It fascinated me to know what went on in the shadier parts of our world. (Most of what he said I still didn't believe.) I hadn't ventured into subearth then. Not many Uppers had. If they did it was for nefarious reasons. But then I went down. And down.

The doctor (the ex-doctor), Alfred Krenz, told me how occasionally, very occasionally Upper women were impregnated by subs - either through relations or rape. They knew the score. They had to go underground. As I was going underground. And the doctor did admit to growing spare body parts from sub-tissue. Though every Upper thought (and quickly buried this thought) that the Officers (the inner government) and the Eloluc (the high government) were receiving organically grown replacement organs and limbs - we never thought things completely through – that logic could not be allowed. And why the hell should we have? We didn't want to be cast out. There were stories of Uppers being thrown to the mercy of the subs if they asked too many questions. I could imagine their fate more than most.

When I got to see the doctor the balance of power between us had shifted. I could tell by his attitude. I could tell as soon as I showed him my toe and described the numbness that was creeping up my leg. But we had a kind of affection for each other. We shared some of the horror of a linked fate. Doctor Krenz lived his life cutting open scarred people. His house and the treatment rooms reminded me more of the subs' houses than our own. Yet there was a certain pleasurable grimness about him. I thought he enjoyed his shadowy life in some strange way.

We greeted.

'Doctor.'

He nodded, did not - for security reasons - refer to me by my full name, and hardly by name at all. Intelligent, haunted eyes examined me behind the circular lenses of his glasses.

'It's strange that we meet this way,' I said.

'Life is strange.'

'You understand why I'm here?'

'You're not the first,' he smiled. Suddenly his slightly pudgy features were ignited in a kind of cold warmth.

My big toe was revealed. As he pricked away at the skin I learnt to my deepening horror that the toe next to it had also lost feeling. My ankle was dulled of life.

'What is the Life Code?' he asked.

'To exist; to maintain the laws; not to transgress the laws; to credate (which meant to accrue wealth, especially for shots); to increase (to have children); to know one's boundary.'

'Good.'

I looked hard at him.

'You're not losing it yet, there's enough time. Do you know about the disease?'

'Yes.'

'What do you know?'

'What I've seen, what I've been told - down there.'

'Did they tell you about the mind?'

I said nothing - wanted to know everything.

'The slow deterioration of the mind...the forgetting of a word; the mixing-up of syllables; stuttering; thinking things you'd rather not think...'

'Are you enjoying this?'

He shook his head. Strands of almost white-blond hair were stretched back across his skull.

'Then why are you telling me?'

'To prepare you.'

'For the worst?' I blurted.

'For the worst.'

'How do you know all this?'

'You know you're not the first,' he laughed. I had not seen him bare his teeth before and I noticed they were discoloured and rather small.

'They've come to me when it's been too late. When the visions had pressed down on their sleeping brains. Nightmares. When they had tried to act normally with their numbed flesh. Smiling; hiding the fact that boiling water had spilt onto their skin – feigning pain if caught. Blaming cuts and scabs on other diseases. Saying nonsense and making it all a joke. Then running. Running away too late. Running to me too late.'

'Am I too late?' I asked bravely.

'I don't know.' He carried on, 'And they wouldn't have the credits to pay...' He seemed to have a new habit – he rolled his head as if his neck ached.

'I...' I began.

He smiled again. 'I do know something else you must prepare for.' His face became serious and his neck stiff.

'What?'

'The Catcher,' he replied.

After some moments I asked coldly, 'The Catcher?'

'You know, you must know - you work for the Register.'

'I work *on* the Register,' I said with some anger.

'Either way,' he smiled, 'you know about The Catcher.'

'But that stuff isn't true.'

'You try it. You'll see. What happens to all those that run? Think your government's let them disappear? You know better than that.'

'I know what happens to the children - that's all.'

'Come off it. What you do to the children is bad enough but at least it's quick I suppose?' Again he rolled his neck nervously.

'We can't take risks...'

'You could check them out, put them in quarantine, give them shots, flush out the bad blood - if there *was* any. Spare them from the rooms...Give them a chance – they're children for dag's sake.'

I thought about what the ex-doctor had said. I hadn't expected this kind of compassion from him. But it only needed one mutation, one chance cross-over into our world and we would be...He was wrong – he must have known he was *wrong*. What we did was cruel, I realised, but cruel for a good reason. That's the way it had always been explained. If the disease mutated in such a way that it could be spread by mucus - then the common cold would wipe us out. Wipe out even the subs. Wipe out every child. Yet I had allowed a little baby to get through the system. Why just him? Why not *every* child? Inside I felt both bad and good.

'No. The disease is virulent, you know. Anything could happen. No risks.'

'What about the Uppers who go down, eh? What about the transgressors who hold good government jobs? What about *you*?'

'Haven't I paid the price?' I shouted. 'I'm not sure anymore - not sure. Everything seemed simple enough not so long ago.'

'But you think the government lets the transgressors slip away?'

'Some. What difference does it make if they're doomed to subearth? That's what happens to them, ripped apart, I know...'

'Yes,' he paused, 'you've been down there...'

'How else?'

'The disease is here, it's with us already, I've told you - you know that's the way I make my money; mostly. If it's going to mutate it's going to mutate...' His eyes pinned me.

'And you don't care?'

'Why should I?' Again he rolled his neck.

'I should have...' I stopped myself quickly and thought how I should have shopped him.

'Listen,' he said, 'the shots that are being sold now, in ten years - probably less - they'll be useless. They'll offer no protection. Your child will be exposed.'

'No.'

'Yes. You want to know something?'

'What?' I spat.

'This government, your government, is already experimenting on subs.'

'No.'

'It's true. I know. Believe me or not. I'm useful sometimes. That's how I live. The Register comes in handy sometimes. Some of the babies don't even enter the White Rooms; or they enter their own special White Rooms.'

'You've never said, mentioned, anything like this before, I don't believe you.'

'Who cares what you know now? I'll try and save you but you'll never see things the same way, will you? And you'll want to protect your child.' A hand swept a loose strand of hair backwards.

I could hardly believe his words.

'The government regularly experiments on the subs; it's looking for a stronger shot. It uses the end-subs and some of the babies whose only fault is to have been born. And the transgressors you track down. The ones that run are even more useful to the government. Uppers with the disease are valued. And that's where Mr. Catcher comes in. And his beasties. *Raths*. And you know too, those little things don't even kill you. Not if you're an Upper. No. When they cut you up and examine the spread of the disease, those bits of you that can still feel, those bits of your brain that can still think are aware of it all. You see how more humane it is to use the end-subs?'

For a while I just sat. I was diseased. I needed a cure. I needed Doctor Alfred Krenz more than ever. The myth of The Catcher was reality. The crawlies; the beasties; the *raths*; they were true. Yet I could hardly believe. But the power between us was all with him. I only had an act of generosity between me and...And even that act was probably futile. This doctor was probably fully known to security. At least I could not call his bluff.

'Will you help me?'

'Yes.'

'Why?'

The doctor went silent suddenly.

'Why?' I repeated.

'Because, you know the truth. You can change things.'

'How?'

'You can - like me - lessen the suffering.' He paused a moment. Seemed wistful, then pulled-himself back to "reality". 'The problem is to attack the disease simultaneously,' he said. 'We have to stop the spread through the body and through the chemicals of the brain. We have to hide the damage so far. Your wife isn't suspicious?'

'No. Not about a disease...'

'Good. Now tell me something else,' he began, 'why were you in subearth - how did you get the disease?'

'I was bitten. I didn't transgress. It must have been a crawlie, a damn spider, a dag arachnid; not a beastie.'

'No, not a beastie. A beastie's bite would have spread quicker and you'd have been tracked down. You're lucky,' he smiled. 'Maybe I can stop the effect of a crawlie; it's easier than the poisoned blood of a sub. And?'

'And?'

'Why were you there?'

'It's another story,' I began.

'Lie down. I'm going to have to do some more cuts; use things that are going to hurt. Hurt when they find the borders of feeling. And I'm going to have to inject some stuff into your brain...'

'No,' I said.

'Tell me your story, concentrate. Tell me your story while I get things prepared. I haven't much to knock you out. I need you half with me. I need to hear the workings of your mind. Listen, you're lucky, remember. No credits, I said. The disease is relatively fresh. But you have to be brave. Your old life has gone Adam X.'

And he used my name for the first time.

'Be strong. Take the pain now, while you can.'

As he approached with the length of fibre-thin needle I began to blurt out my story. Sweat soaked my skin. The needle kissed my flesh.

When I came round I was in a different room and strapped to a hard surface. Pain seemed to travel in waves down my leg and my mind kept piecing together an image. An image some other portion of my brain could not comprehend. Being strapped down I was unable to see anything other than the ceiling above. Bending my fingers brought good blood flow. My toes only partially responded. Blood travelled slowly through my ankle. And an intense pain throbbed in both feet. Eventually I managed to curl most of my toes. But a wave of pain lapped around the numbness - and for a moment, an intense lightning moment, I felt the contour of my dead toes too.

My forehead was strapped down as were my feet and wrists. A strap pressed across and against my chest and upper arms. Moving as much of my body as I could I also felt a restriction across my thighs. But it was the curious waves of images through my mind that frightened me and made me feel nauseous. Fragmentary pieces of a particular image swam in confusion. Blinking my eyes I concentrated on a crack running across the ceiling.

Pain expressed in thoughts becomes abstract. But with the reassembling of the picture in my mind came the *memory* of pain. Except the memory could only be found through metaphor. The thought of the pain made me shudder inside the straps. But to describe it...it was like having been turned inside out and the guts and organs squashed by rough hands. It was like a razor sharp needle piercing an unblinking eye.

But not only was there the extremity of pain, there had been its continuance also. I wasn't even sure if the pain was real or imaginary - it didn't matter. Perhaps my brain had been probed? The sense of the pain existing for time-stretched was harder for me to capture. It seemed as if when one prolonged sting became too much I had shifted (mentally or physically) into the merest fragment of relief. Then a different but equally terrible pain would engulf me.

How physical is any pain? Yes we feel - but *where* do we feel? The body's hurt is managed by the mind. The mind is terrified, the body suffers. And when the pain is finished then the bodily pain is quickly usurped by its painful memory.

The image in my mind was forming well enough for me to see the contour of a face. And then to see that the face was female. By then localised pain was throbbing warmly around the base of my big toe where foot-flesh existed. And pain washed in from the top of my ankles. Both feet ached. The face kept sharpening its image. The face kept blurring and focusing. Pulsating in my mind. The pain I felt then was transmitted to my stomach. I felt nauseous. I wanted to rip open my belly and pull out the shit. I wanted to empty my belly of everything - and uncoil the intestines. The sick feeling seemed eternal.

And then the absolute terror of being held restricted hit me. And that was the worst hurt of all. But, it seemed, the moment of this realisation brought the face to clarity. And it was Zee. It was Zee who was watching me from within my mind. And some part of me was watching her watching me. Zee. Implacable. Inscrutable. Deep eyes. Bold and strongly delineated. Zee. Inside me.

Doctor Krenz came looming over my terrified eyes. 'Finished,' he said.

'Finished?'

'Yes.'

'And?' I asked, sweating.

'And? You mean, has it worked? I don't know.'

'When will you know?' I said pulling at my restraints.

'I don't know.'

'Release me,' I said.

'But it isn't finished,' he said.

'But you said it was finished.'

'That part,' he said, rolling his neck.

'Which part?'

'The first part,' he said.

'No more, please, no more.'

'This is nothing,' he said, 'nothing to the pain of the disease.'

I was helpless. He disappeared from my vision. My heart was racing and my lips dry. I could feel my heart swollen and itching. Then he came back.

'This won't hurt as bad,' he said.

My eye watched the needle turn from its long, thin shaft into an invisible point. I sensed the point come close to my eyeball and then the infinity of pain. A grain of sand was rubbed into the eye of my mind.

Chapter 8

A week later I went back to see "Doctor" Krenz. I had been drinking. With debts mounting and no credits coming in I drank away my wife's resources. I didn't use up her shot-stack nor my kid's insurance money – at least I had the good sense to arrange that. Not even I was that much of a bastard. And the funny thing? I had been offered promotion at work. I went along with it all, but what did it mean? I knew the whole business was a sham. A dag. I would never be part of the real government - I was one of their many puppets. Doing their dirty work. Keeping the Register going. Sending the innocents to the slaughter. Little babies and children to the White Rooms. What a wonderful little nursery for the Upper bastards.

'News?' I asked.

'Well,' he said, 'how do you feel?'

'I can't feel my right ankle fully, I'm beginning to limp, I have to correct myself. I have to guard myself or make small excuses. I'm protected by my position - of course. And by my meaningless contacts. Also by my reputation, and now growing reputation, of alcohol consumption. Perhaps I should start calling it "grog" consumption? So, I don't feel so well, doctor. News?'

'You'll need money,' he said, taking off his glasses and wiping his circular lenses.

'Money?'

'Money. Credits. Cheque-assurance.'

'I haven't got any credits. That's why I'm here. No credits, no mon-ey, no cheques; no insurance stash; no dob (the old-fashioned word for credits before money came back into popular slang-speech).'

'No money,' the doctor said. 'I'm not talking full-price,' he said.

'I'm talking noth-ing,' I said.

'Then there is a problem. It hasn't worked…'

'Really?' I asked sarcastically.

Ignoring my tone he carried on, 'You've got to get a shot, a lot of shot - it's the only way. Or there is...'

'What?'

'A desperate way.'

'Which is?'

'Get as much shot as you can and then you cut off the bad flesh.'

'What?'

'Cut off the bad flesh. The shot goes further, less to go in,' he joked, 'and there's a chance the spread will be stemmed. The mind can fight itself. I've seen it done. Your mind seems sharp enough – perhaps that worked. The disease is contained within the bad flesh. I've done it before.'

'And with what kind of success?'

'Not so good. Some have been cured bodily, but mentally...'

'Where, where are all these people, if it's true?'

'Thrown into subearth. Disposed of. Disappeared. It's easy enough, you know that.'

'I don't believe it.'

'As you please. It's all academic unless you've got some credit. You have credated in the past, haven't you?'

After some deep thought I said to him, 'Look, can't you lend me some credit? I'll get you off the Register...'

'I'm not on,' he laughed.

'I'll get you back into things, I know people...'

'Save it. I'll do my best for you. Can't promise much more. But I've got no money spare...' Krenz rolled his neck then rubbed it with his right hand.

Two weeks after the dinner party and its aftermath, which confirmed my fate I was sitting weeping in the doctor's arms. Life had indeed ended.

At home I could hardly bare the happiness of my wife. She seemed oblivious to the financial plight we were in. Spent her time talking about the baby and how our future would be. She even gave up trying to stop me drinking – or asking me "difficult" questions. She let me do what and how I wished. But all I did was work and drink and sleep in fitful nightmares. My mind and body deteriorated - as a result of the disease or my depression I did not know. Then one night a helper came to me when I was alone.

'We know you're in trouble,' he said.

'What's your business here? It's late. You know you're not to address me so.'

'We know you're in trouble.'

'What trouble?'

'Zee. The baby. And now...'

'Now what?'

'The way you move. We know, we understand, we can *smell* it.'

It was the end for me. Psychologically I was terrified of the disease spreading - and of some slow death. Some living death. My nightmares played out the same scene – I could see myself laid out on a mortuary slab for dead, but with my eyes twitching alive; my body unable to move. I needed money. I needed some shot. And then, in my own home, my final authority was dismissed.

'We know where she is.'

'Who?'

'We know.'

'Why are you telling me?'

'You can help us.'

'Help *you*? I can't help you and I don't need your help.'

'Yes you do.'

I thought quickly. I was at the end of my tether. 'Tell me what you want,' I blurted.

'Get myself and one other papers and we'll tell you where she is and when she's meeting him.'

'Him?'

'The man she *transgressed* with.'

Again I thought quickly, 'Okay. I'll do it. I can do it.' I sweated.

And thus was my fate sealed entirely.

Getting the papers wouldn't be too difficult by I didn't know if they would actually work or not. I no longer knew what was valid in the world I had so recently felt so comfortable in. A world I thought I understood and had control of. A world that was an hallucination. If the papers worked they – these "helpers" - would be as free as I was enslaved.

Later that night I hugged my wife and told her how much I loved her. And the curious thing was that I loved her more then than at any time before. I began to see qualities in her I had never before witnessed. Her tolerance of my excess; her loyalty; her devotion...

At a secret meeting with the helper who had approached me I handed over the papers; I received from him all the details I needed. Simple. Clear cut. I was about to step out of safety. I had the disease - I was on the path to death, and hell was a way-station (and didn't I just laugh at the thought of that - its closeness in sound to Wayland). How simple life can be when there are no options.

I left a note for my wife and my as yet unborn child. I tried to explain as much as I could - but not enough to condemn her. I hoped I could sort out my "troubles" and right all the wrongs. What would she think? She would think a thousand things. But I didn't want them kicked down into subearth. By leaving, by vanishing, I hoped to cover my diseased path.

On the way to subearth I called at Doctor Krenz's. He laughed when I told him about the helpers. Thought I was a fool to trust them. But I grabbed him by the throat and told him I would be back - I would have enough credit for a huge shot - a shot no disease could fight. And then I would take my wife and make a life anew.

He said mockingly, 'Where?'

By the coast, by the sanatoria - get over to one of the islands.'

'They'll never let you. You're stigmatised. You're corrupted. The government won't let you live. The Catcher will find you.'

As I looked into his eyes then, I hated him.

Leaving everything behind, I took the car and hissed my way through the twinkling city. Everything took on a sharpness. Everything I saw I ached to have to leave. There was a technological splendour about Upper. If you didn't ask questions, then the Upper world was a beautiful place. I cursed Zee and her unknown lover for bringing me to this. I cursed the government for its falsity. I cursed the subs for their white, lifeless bodies. I cursed the crawlies. I cursed the rat-infested houses where I had gone and the room where I had slept. And all the while I heard the buzzing of a wasp as if it were in the car with me.

Before long I knew I would be listed missing. Then the questions would come. If my wife had the grace to cover for me I might last two days - four into the weekend (and I had enough luck to be on a waver that weekend). Yes, if I was lucky I had four days. (Uppers often used di for day – there had been a change in the calendar many years previously.) And in my hand I clutched the address and map written and drawn on shiny paper. And there was the time they would meet - those lovers. My "helpers" (now ex) seemed to know much about Zee's goings on. There was a world within a world in Upper. Being un-used to holding written material forced my neglected fingernails into the palms of my hands - so that blood oozed.

Before I reached the border, with the wind whistling across from the southern plains, I transferred to my digital, went to burn the paper but decided to secrete it in a tight trouser pocket. Taking the digital from my wrist I opened my jacket and shirt and taped it to my chest. It was a smart move. This was the only thing between sanity and madness. It was cold outside. The last month (sector) of the year had begun. The Exmass obsession was biting in the Upper world - though that close to the border it seemed as if I had already left.

I crossed at a different border from usual. The fence between Upper and subearth stretched for lengths into the distance. Cutting the land in two - a permanent scar. Traders sold black swag in shanty stalls on the subearth side. Crossing at that lower border meant a long detour and a longer drive to pick up the main earth road. There were only a series of tracks that connected the different roads to the crossings. The motor hissed pulling and lifting the car's body as far from the potholes and rocks as it could.

I noticed the farmsteads for the first time. The sheds I took to be the animal houses. And I noticed the poverty, the ramshackle nature of the subs' housing. The dilapidation of the farm buildings. It got even worse on the south side, so I had been told. I also thought about the mystery lands that Zee had mentioned. And I thought about my wife at home.

Dropping the motor as close to Wayland as I dared I quickly camouflaged the body and got changed. This time I carried a shooter. It came from Jo's father. It wasn't "state of the art" but I figured it might do the job and it had live shells. I remembered Zee carrying fire. When things blew I knew the tirade Jo could expect from her father. Wouldn't the old man be proved right? I also imagined the recriminations in the office. The accusations. The *one person* who would be asking himself questions - that is if he hadn't also disappeared for good by then (the dag arachnid). But I had four days to sort things out; a slim chance, but a chance nevertheless.

The wind forced me to stoop as I headed for the town. Great banks of dirty-grey clouds scudded through the air. This air smelt different - the light was different. I thought of happier times back in Upper. Of the serenity I (we) had found in weekend retreats. Back in Upper I recalled trips to the coast, near the sanatoria where the neurotics and pimps went. Where the underhand business was carried on. But it had only been mild stuff. Hadn't affected us.

As I walked I thought about the children I had condemned to the White Rooms. Babies like Adam had been signed over to their death. I knew what happened there. Most Uppers who took any notice of anything knew. For dag's sake we knew. But still there were the myths - the myths of the "Saintly Children", carried by winged and sailed boats to the islands. The islands off the coast, in the mist, shrouded in denser legend. Islands that, in fact, were the homes to the convicts, typhoid and diphtheria - to small pox and the new-death (a disease preferable to *the* disease). The disease none had named was kept to the subs. Kept to the subs and the White Rooms. And to the Uppers who went down.

I thought about all those who I had put on the Register, thinking only exile to subearth was their destiny. If the ex-doctor was correct then they were all hunted down. Perhaps even the tales of the catchers were true. We lived in a world where so much good was being done that I found it hard to think of a darker alternative. But it was also true that the Eloluc (the elite members of the founding Upper families; high government and military) were in constant perfect health, mind and body. All of us knew about the grown body-parts - but perhaps something more sinister was going on? Upper was a world of schizophrenics.

Once I had hoped to be an Eloluc. Jo's father had missed his chance because he had married out. And perhaps he had been over-zealous on his campaigns. But the Upper world worked. It ran smoothly, it kept out the disease. And if one thinks logically then it was better that the children went to the White Rooms rather than...went through the anguish of the disease itself. This was the way I thought. As cold as the wind that blew. Little had I realised that I could never be an Eloluc.

Casting my mind back to the long-huts, I saw again the rows of perfect bodies and trapped eyes. But this time as I looked down on their faces; each frozen face was a face I knew. I stopped briefly, checked the digital for information. How was it that the helpers were allowed to serve but the children were...were, "evacuated"? This thought ran through my head, yet I knew the answer. The helpers had never developed the disease; could sniff out the crawlies; the children could have had the disease without anyone knowing. It was the stuff of nightmares, but true. The children could harbour the disease for their first five years without showing symptoms. We knew. Before the split into the two worlds, mothers who gave milk passed on the disease - mothers who had the disease passed it to their children. Blood got into the chain from routine blood tests and inoculations (when needles were more commonly used). Accidents happened.

Children bit and scratched. Children fought. It only needed one incident to get into the sex-chain and...I took a deep breath. Part of my family had died as a result of one such spread. Before the split these things were not uncommon. Before the split every resource was used. And then it seemed simple - to divide, to separate. We had been separated for a long, long time.

The divide was further deepened by the wars. By the time of the Legionnaires we were distinct. But it seemed the best, the fairest way - the most humane. Those who were infected, or related, or disagreed, became the subs. The Uppers were left. And at least we kept things clean. And we helped the subs by taking helpers. Monitoring. Giving money. Resources. Much. And didn't all we ask, was for their people and our people to respect the Laws? Yet some transgressed and threatened everything.

When I became a government official, working in Records and on the Register it was the greatest day of my life. I was keeping the faith. I was keeping the Laws. I was protecting all of us. All of our people - and their people. If it meant children going to the White Rooms then the end justified the means. To be truthful in all my years there had only been hundreds, not thousands of cases. Before the split a chain could have killed many thousands. Only one chain. Chains are meant to be broken. I was doing my job. *And I lost it.*

Getting close to the town I reminded myself of the look in Zee's eyes. As I recalled the night we spent together a part of me knew that my weakness, my recklessness, would risk all again. But I couldn't explain this. It went beyond the lust for her body; beyond the love for my wife and unborn child; beyond the service to my world. It went beyond my own rationale. I did what I did for reasons I could have justified at the time but, truly, I did what I did because it had been my *instinct.*

The sun shone weakly as great balls of cloud diffused its glow. In the outskirts of the town the same flotsam and jetsam of the vacant minded and twisted bodies floated in the rat-infested streets. Turning one corner I watched a sub with rats clinging onto her dead ankle flesh. But life still flowed. The everyday chores of life continued. Smells of cooking permeated the air. The braziers burnt. Children played. Wasps crawled over the detritus left lying in the scuttling gutters; gutters alive with brown furred filth. Smoke rose from chimneys. Washing was hung out to dry. Street games were played by limbless men. The able-bodied spat on the dying. Life went on.

And as I rounded a sewer-stinking corner a clammy hand must have reached out. Caught by its cold clench I was dragged into a crumbling building. Something thudding at the back of my skull took away all thought.

Chapter 9

The Catcher's eyes flicked open. Someone had reported Adam X. A file had been opened; a person from the Register Affairs, Records, had either been telling lies or knew something damning about Adam X.

'Do we wait or simply leave it?' a government voice asked.

The Eloluc were represented. 'We shouldn't take any chances.'

The Catcher sat impassively. Known by his generic title he would respond only when directly addressed. For the time being he was content to play with the beastie, the *rath* inside his jacket pocket.

'If we decide to go ahead then we have to eliminate. If we decide to go ahead without full authority...'

'Or evidence,' the Eloluc butted in.

'Then it has to be in subearth and all traces covered. The father-in-law has influence. No bringing back - too dangerous.'

The Eloluc glanced at the official.

'So?' the Head asked.

'He has certainly transgressed.'

'He might even have the disease. Get rid of him,' said the second official.

The Head turned to The Catcher, 'What do you recommend orla (this was the usual form of address to a catcher by a high-government representative or official)?

The Catcher squeezed a smile from his thin lips. 'Kill.'

'Justify,' said the Eloluc.

'If he dies or if he lives makes no difference. Because he works on the Register; because of his family, then if he has the disease it is my duty to exterminate. If he has transgressed he has no further role. If he is innocent he will have lost authority.'

'But the Commander..?' (Referring to Adam's father-in-law.)

'If traces are covered he will not care,' said The Catcher.

'You hear the orla's words,' said the Head. 'We must act; either way.'

'I will make him speak,' said The Catcher, 'you have not to have fear. His confession will expose any chains. Expose anything rotten inside Records.'

'Then let it be so,' said the Eloluc. 'We support.'

'And my officials?' asked the Head.

They nodded.

The Catcher moved silently, exhausted by his words. He was in a short temper having lost for the first time that year white-bodying.

'Make him speak,' said the Head.

'He will speak. And then he will die.'

The Catcher was mildly interested in Adam X. the Register official. He was not Eloluc, he was not high-government, but if he had transgressed then he was a cancer at the body's heart. An interesting case perhaps; and married to a commander's daughter. The evidence against him could go either way. But he, The Catcher, would first take his words and then take his life. Or rather the *rath* would.

At his home, The Catcher went to the sealed back room. It was here that he studied, bred and genetically engineered/modified the beasties. His love for the brown crawly things had developed from an early boyhood passion. Whereas others hunted for spiders and diligently killed them, The Catcher had broken the laws and captured them. In those days there were still some to be found in the Upper north-eastern valleys. All spiders were suspect of course. But of the millions that had been poisoned or killed in a multitude of ways, only a handful carried the disease. The Catcher had needed only two to breed. Eventually even the breeding scheme was made redundant.

The Catcher loved his stubby-legged, plump bodied creatures. Loved the webs they made - though the web for them was anachronistic; a work of art. The web was to the spider what a piece of art or sculpture was to a human in the Upper world.

To begin he had bred the spiders. Handling them with heavy gloves and keeping them in lead-sealed glass cases. Later he gained their trust - instinctively, perhaps more; they did not bite him. The spiders carried the disease as a result of a terrible accident. Genetic experiments had produced an unlucky cross-over into the insect world, contaminating the common house fly. The fly reproduced and mutated the disease quickly, but it was the spiders that ate them that developed a reaction and a liquid which hosted the disease. Nobody for sure knew whether the disease was a mixture of a natural and dormant substance or purely a synthetic disease - or a combination of the two. The flies had lain eggs in a butchered calf which had been genetically altered and which (unknown to the original scientists) had been infected by TLP - a disease traceable to NLD.

The spiders (*rapithra thufri*) turned aggressive and began biting people. And then the terrible disease passed to humans. Chains developed and grew; link by link. The Catcher became fascinated by spiders in general and by the *"raths"* in particular. But all spiders were hunted and killed. Killed by all manner of means. And much later, in subearth, those forefathers of the modern disease-free helpers developed the sniff. And with the sniff they tracked and killed the spiders who survived in grim hiding places. Wasps and rats were bred to help exterminate the spiders. (The practice of keeping a wasp in the home being a subearth tradition that survived.) But in subearth the species survived. In Upper, the fear survived (and there were those who maintained the myth that diseased spiders still existed).

The Catcher had found his *raths* in the valleys but it was his later cloning of these and their non-organic adaptation that led to them becoming beasties not crawlies. It was from The Catcher that the development of semi-robotic insects was used for military purposes; though never officially. It was The Catcher who created the hunter-*raths*. He had done all that from a boyhood passion. And since he'd begun there were now twenty catchers operating for the government. And though their status was semi-mystical, The Catcher knew well enough their record. They did not fail. They hunted with their beasties and brought in their prey. Those Uppers who escaped below were reduced to the living dead. Captured and brought back to be experimented on or killed. Any subs were automatically exterminated. The catchers were rightly feared.

The spiders The Catcher produced were formidable creatures. They had highly developed hunting skills - a tenacity that could see them cover scores of lengths to kill their prey. They had resilience to all predators and because of their robotic components could survive most natural adversities (though submersion in water was sometimes a problem). Even when the organic spider died the robotic could survive. The Catcher did not control these beings in any truly mechanical sense but rather had developed a relationship. He was able to train other catchers in developing this relationship. It was linked in some way to the ancient art of horse-whispering. A skill now as dead as the horses of old (the only horses remaining being those flogged near half to death in subearth).

Spider communication was based on holding a pre-modified beast in the palm of the hand (known as a crawlie - many humans had died in training) and creating a subtle interaction through movements of the hand muscles and the spider's reaction to the palm's sweat. Breath is also blown over the *rath*. Nothing concrete is known about how the feeling is achieved. Only The Catcher has exact knowledge. One day – he promised - he would pass this knowledge on.

The Catcher loved his beasts. Loved them in a way he could not his fellow men and women. He had mild distaste for Uppers and contempt for subs. Of the subs with the disease he had no emotion whatsoever. Only when he witnessed the white-bodying did he display a flicker of concern, but this was not for the fate of the stoners, only the credits he had heaped on either.

The Catcher exhausted the computer files on Adam X. Paid a visit to the man's home - spied on his pregnant wife. When he was ready he chose the beastie. When the crawling body was dropped into his pocket he took a vehicle from the compound and headed for subearth. No questions. No further inquiry. Adam X. had been missing for two days and his guilt shone.

As the engine hissed through the Upper world The Catcher reminded himself of the sport, white-bodying, he so enjoyed. He also cursed himself for losing, wondered why he had chosen the snake over the turtle on his last visit. Wondered too how men - like the man upon whom he was preying - could have lead the lives of government officials. Thinking about Adam he wondered exactly what the particular nature of his descent was. Thought how each link of this man's fallen life would have to be reanimated to trace those connected. The spy in the Register Affairs would also, eventually, be hunted. The wife of Adam would be persecuted. The Commander would fall from historical grace - be written out of history as was the norm.

From these traces they would find others. And these others would lead to yet more others. For it was imperative to keep the Upper world pure in mind and deed - which meant hunting down the unclean ones.

At the border the zealous guards stopped him.

'Identification.'

The Catcher smiled.

'Identification,' the middle-aged one snapped.

The Catcher flicked open his digital. Their look. Oh, how it amused him.

'Carry on through,' the unshaven face grovelled.

Yes he would. Oh yes he would. And did they know what he carried in his pocket? A beautiful creature that could bite them dead in an instant - or bite them into a near eternity. Whatever, in fact, he - The Catcher chose.

On into subearth he hissed. With his right hand he tickled the beastie. Began to communicate with it. And this was a thrill The Catcher never tired of. Began to lock into the memory of a species that was so different from the human. A creature that had a perfect and yet terrible beauty. A creature that had bolted onto its living insect-limbs the most superb technology of the Uppers.

The Catcher sang to the beastie in his jacket pocket; sang with the twitch of muscle and skin; sang with the moistening of his palms;

sang with the leaking DNA and the melding of two life forms - and the inaudible throbbing of microscopic science.

One day science would end their dependence upon the subs. One day there would be no need of the organic. One day there would be no shadowy movement from the long-huts of subearth to the cloying politeness of the corridors of power of the Eloluc.

The wind of the day before had settled down. The Catcher smiled. There were twenty others of his kind hunting as he. They never tired; they were always needed. It was the way of things. The likes of Adam X. were bad apples dropping from the tree of life. And the tree stood in Upper paradise. For the world of the Uppers *was* paradise. So long, of course, as you did not transgress the laws.

Chapter 10

When I slowly came round I discovered my hands and feet were tied. Struggling momentarily, I could hear the voices of at least two men close by. The place stank. An ache throbbed at the back of my head and I felt sick. I could taste vomit in my throat and my chest hurt. My instinct was to keep trying to wriggle out of the knots but a second, perhaps even deeper instinct, caused me to still - survival. I could feel the fire-piece wedged inside the back of my trousers; having it reassured me but I knew if they found it, it could also prove serious trouble. It meant whoever had bound me wasn't that smart either.

Without moving at all I listened to the voices.

'Wese'll have to make a decision soon,' came one.

'Yes, yes, I know...'

'We could kill him the old fashioned way, youse understand? Into the...' I heard laughter.

'But he must be alive - he's no use dead; and him gonna make us big dob.'

'Youse got in touch with them shellin' Uppers - them robbers?'

'Aye.'

'Theyse want him "on the hoof" for big dob…'

'We could smash him out again...'

'Too dangerous. Them'll not give out for a bad-un.'

'Them'll have to come 'ere, see and do with him. Give us big credit.'

'He ain't no spy or nought, he ain't no trainer on the look out?' (For "stoners", I imagined – and I was learning fast.) The voice continued, 'We ain't bein' tricked 'ere?'

'No. Sniff him. Nothing. Him on the run all right.'

'You sure him's perfect?'

'Course I be.'

'You looked all over? Youse searched him?'

'Tapped im down. You see him too.'

'We'll strip him when the robbers come...'

'No. Wese gotta meet up at the pig-pens…'

I heard more laughter.

I was terrified and curious simultaneously. They wanted me in perfect shape. I was not. They had not witnessed my slight limp – seen my ankle, thank holy-fuck. But what exactly they had in mind I could not decide. But I had ideas. Though they had "tapped" me down they had missed the fire; missed its slender bullets; missed the digital – missed everything! They were either stupid or in a hurry. One of them came back in the room where I was held and I slumped back out of consciousness - or so it would have seemed. I thanked their sloppiness – were they infected by the disease perhaps?

'The bastard, he out?'

'Him out.'

A hand touched my face - the smell from its skin was almost overwhelming. But I had to keep loose and still.

'He have a pretty face, eh? Face soft.'

The other voice I had heard came into the room also. As it talked I heard it grow louder and close.

'A face which anna been wiped, eh?'

'No reason. Got him his nose and ears, and eyes – like a dag helper. Pull them beautiful things open...'

Trying not to react in panic I let the rough fingers spring my lids apart and I desperately focused into nothingness, letting my pupils drop.

'We should see what him's like as a man, eh?'

'What you'n mean?'

'See if he ain't rubbed nothin' else away.'

They laughed again.

Then a terrible scream came from outside and I felt their attention trapped - I almost gave myself away by taking too quick a breath.

'What beent?'

'Take a look.'

A voice came more distant but I could still smell the rank odour of a face close to mine.

'Them's got a chimp. Quick now. Them got a chimp.'

The rankness faded.

'They gonna burn him?'

'*We* gonna burn him,' the first voice shouted.

'Let's go.'

'What about this un?'

'Him's out for a while, and he ain't goin' nowhere. Wese be back soon enough. You want to see the chimp burn or not? Him real big.'

I waited till they hadn't spoken for some time. Fear kept my eyes closed. But a sensation forced me to risk opening them - and it was the strength of survival again. The floor I lay on sweated with stale urine and crawled with slimy insects. They had half-propped me up but nevertheless it was difficult and painful to get to my feet. Before I could do so I rolled against the floor and my face stuck to its greasy surface. The back of my head flared up in a lightning strike of pain. But all my will gave both leg and stomach muscles the power to raise me.

Standing up I looked about the dark and dirty room. Heading for a doorway away from where I thought the subs had left, I hobbled over debris. As quickly and as carefully as I could I jumped over some piled bricks and through the empty door frame. The next room had no doors, was small, but there was a window without its glass on the right-hand wall.

Instinctively I went to below where the light shone. I was sweating with fear and occasional strikes of pain shot down the back of my skull. There was a loosening of my bowels too - those men meant business. Rubble from the window allowed me enough height to peek through. The view gave out onto the side of another brick building, but I heard the scream of animal and sub from the distance. As I shifted my tied ankles I felt the crack of glass, and it was this that gave me the idea to free myself. Sitting down on the rubble I pulled my arms to one side and forced the rope onto the edge of a shard of glass. Slowly I rubbed against it. It seemed an eternity before the rope shredded and my wrists became free. As I pulled my arms loose I could see a trail of blood. This pleased me. Though the cut was sharp and deep I was glad that my blood ran clean.

As I freed my ankles and then took a "nose-blow" to the wound I heard a sound from the next room. At least one of the men must have come back to check on me. Sweat soaked my skin. With adrenaline stiffening my bad ankle I hoisted myself up onto the ledge of the rotting wooden frame and heaved myself through. As I landed the other side I heard the grunt of one of the men. I went to run away but as I backed against the brick wall I felt the shape of the fire. A plan took hold.

I let the sub see me run back into the building next to where I had been caught. Inside there I waited for him. He had called for no assistance and so I let his arrogance catch him out. As he headed through the doorway I struck him hard on the crown of his head with the butt of the pistol. It saved a bullet. But he wasn't knocked out. The sub began to mouth words and gained strength in his voice. But I shoved the fire into the side of his nose by his piggy eye and said:

'Start speaking you bastard, who are you?'

He wouldn't say anything at first but I told him I had nothing to lose and began to squeeze the trigger.

'Speak.'

'You an Upper mister?'

'Who cares?'

'We thoughts you un a sub.'

I thought he was lying – something in his manner. 'What were you going to do with me, eh?' I shoved the pistol nozzle in hard to his flesh.

'Give unt to body snatchers.'

'Who are they?'

He looked genuinely bemused.

'Thems body snatchers...'

'You were going to give me to them?'

He nodded.

'Alive?'

He nodded again.

'What were they going to do?'

Again he looked bemused.

'Tell me,' I shrieked.

'Spare parts,' he mumbled.

'What?'

'Youse pure, youse like an angel. Theyse pay good money for youse limbs and stuff.'

I went to smash his face. The sub almost spewed.

'Where's the other? Eh? Tell me!'

'Thems roasting big chimp.'

'You told the body snatchers?'

He nodded.

'Where are they?'

'We gonna meet them at the outskirts; by the pig-pens...'

'Where?'

'The long-huts, the long-huts, where them piggies live.'

'You mean subs?'

He spat. 'Angels,' he laughed.

'What time?'

'Just afore the sun fall.'

'Which huts?'

'Thems called WSW5. True angel.'

'I should kill you you bastard.'

'No. Wese poor. Wese got it. Wese started. Right enough. We need dob, we need help. Need to escape su.'

I smashed the fire into his temple and he went out cold.

All my fears and suspicions about my world seemed to be true. It was as if I belonged nowhere. There was a trade in limbs from subearth to the Upper world. The Eloluc, with their perfect octogenarian bodies were most likely the recipients. Their explanations seemed so feeble to me now; but it was only recently that I needed to give those explanations much thought. My limbs; my eyes; my brain might have been cut up and stored for further use. And if the doctor was correct I had more to worry about than a couple of sub amateurs. The Catcher and his beasties would make me a zombie. As a zombie I would lie in the long-huts. As a zombie I would be cut up; feel everything from inside my mind. Then I would pray for the disease. Then I would envy the insane ones.

Shaking my thoughts free I looked around the dark room. I needed to escape that part of the town. Needed to find Zee, but I wanted to prove conclusively the words of the sub. I wanted to be at the long-huts when the body snatchers turned up. I wanted to see their ghoulish eyes, find out if they were Uppers or subs. Find out if they hunted stray Uppers too. Maybe do them some damage. I held the fire firmly. The sub lying at my feet made a groan. Quickly and viciously I struck him again. A bruise sat on another bruise and a thin red line of blood trickled from the corner of his right eye. The place brutalised me. In the distance, somewhere outside, a roar erupted from a huge sounding crowd.

I knew I was in danger. The sub grapevine would sound. Limbless creatures would cart themselves from street corner to street corner. Nose-less boys and fingerless girls would rush between the gnarled legs of the adults. Sex subs (body-dealers) would whisper. They knew now that I was on the run - and dangerous - but they didn't know what I looked like. And I had something going for me; I had the disease. Bizarrely, that would help me escape.

Hurrying from the rear of the building (having worked my way through room after dismal room) I stepped into a courtyard. A sub woman with a scar running down her face looked at me suspiciously.

'Ya all reet muffer?' I asked jauntily.

'Greetings to ee,' she replied guardedly.

I limped past her. She turned away.

I didn't know exactly where I was in the town. The late autumn sun (for it was already the last month of the year) dipped behind the crumbling tenements. Fires grew brighter. I exaggerated my limp. A girl came up to me.

'Want a good un?'

I smiled.

'You a nice fuck hun; wanna lie with I?'

I smiled again but kept walking.

'No like I?'

'Youse pretty,' I said, 'but have to find...' I realised I couldn't say where Zee was meant to be hiding out but, instinctively the name, "WSW5" came out.

'What youse awants there?'

'Business,' I said cheerily.

'I'll tells you.'

'Thanks.'

'For a price.'

'How much?'

'Twenty-five.'

'Credits?'

'You can have I for that,' she said pulling down her ragged blouse. I turned away from her dirty breast.

'Here. Tell I.'

And so it was settled that I would go first to the long-huts, from there I planned to sleep outside of Wayland and come back the next day to find Zee. I reckoned by then it would be safer. By then I would know some more of the truth of Upper world. And I had time.

With the girl's directions I limped through the darkening streets. Part of my way led across waste land. The way would save me time and there would be less people, but the girl also warned me that it was the type of landscape adored by chimpanzees.

The faces of the subs I saw all seemed to eye me with suspicion. I avoided their look - avoided the mutilations of the disease. Avoided the shredded flesh. There was a smell of putrefaction in the air that the braziers could not dispel. The night was coming on. Cold was descending as the sun dipped below its distant horizon. I imagined my wife, at home, worried about me. Our child growing, oblivious to the fate of its father.

Heading across the wasteland I took the pistol from my back pocket and held it tight in my sweating hand. Light seemed different in that landscape. The last month (sector) had begun - Exmass loomed. There was an eerie silence and detachment from the horror of the rest of Wayland. It was almost like a graveyard of old - when bodies weren't burnt or disposed of in government chemical plants of eternal rest. Yes I was growing cynical. Cynical about everything except for my wife and baby. Yet it was Zee I was desperate to meet again.

There was a flatness suddenly about the ground I trod across. I stubbed my unfeeling big toe through the soft leather of my shoe. It had been a mistake to wear leather shoes - they marked me out. I dirtied them up some more and sat on a wall that stood out from the general rubble. And it was then that I heard the silence rented. Looking across the wasteland into the distance, with the fires of Wayland burning against the cold blue of the sky or the gathering sunset, I saw it. One lone chimpanzee had raised itself up and was looking in my direction; dropping itself down on to the back of its hands. Even from the distance it was I could see its grinning face and twisted mouth. It shrieked when it saw me get up and more chimpanzees gathered about it. I knew how vicious these animals could be. Especially this mutant strain.

Running as fast as I was able, I could hear the chimps screaming after me. I needed to get to a building. The stones and bricks beneath my feet made running awkward but I could only imagine the chimps gliding over the terrain; their forelimbs hung low, their legs strong.

I didn't want to look behind but the sense that they were catching me up grew overwhelmingly terrifying. My ankle ached and dragged my pace down. As I turned my head to sneak a glance at the beasts I tripped and fell to the floor. My cut hand reopened its wound and I tasted blood and dust in my mouth. The pistol went from my grasp. If I used the gun I knew the subs would be sent crazy. I had to make decisions. I crawled forward to retrieve the pistol. The chimps were scrabbling up close. I was utterly terrified. With the fire in my hand I rolled over with the chimps only a half length away. There was nothing to be done but fire. I let go a shot. The leading chimp was caught on its shoulder. The bullet ripped through the fur and flesh and seemed to burst the shoulder open. Its scream was wild and horrific. It stopped and fell backwards. The other chimps screamed a high pitch squeal and jumped up and down near the stricken creature.

Gathering courage they made to come again, but tentatively this time. I let another shot off and grimaced at the crack it made in the darkening air. There was enough light for me to see steam rising from the chimps' fur. Another chimp was struck - they made an easy target. Part of a head splattered into a frightful mess. All ran. The two I had shot moaned as they retreated slowly – one of them slumping agonisingly into death. I stood up and continued to head for a building opposite.

Inside the stinking building, which smelt of chimpanzee muck, I loaded two bullets into the fire. It shot five, I had three spare. I felt tired. My head ached. Blood seeped continuously from my hand and night was falling. I imagined street gangs of subs looking for the source of the gun fire. I imagined the chimpanzees growing in number. In the end the fear got too much and I knew I had to make a run for it before dark came completely. Rushing from the building I let off two more shots out of panic and ran for my life. I ran until I could hardly breathe. Slumped down in some undergrowth and waited and listened.

Escaping from the bushes I headed back towards houses. I looked out for the chimney the girl had spoken of as a reference. It was close. I had made it. I wasn't far from the long-huts and with luck I knew the body-snatchers would be waiting. The gun was hidden as I limped back into the narrow streets. Keeping an eye on the top of the chimney stack I used it as my bearing. The girl had been worth her money. A band of subs marched down the street with torches blazing. I dipped into a dark doorway. My heart froze. As they passed I heard them shouting. They were chimp hunting it seemed.

I slunked down. I had to keep going. A noise close to me brought back my senses. A rat was sniffing round my right foot. I lashed out and booted its soft body. I spat onto the ground, stood, and pulled myself mentally and physically together. Stepping into the street again I prepared to meet the villains who would have cut me up live - sold me to the Eloluc, or whoever did their dirty work. I was no nearer Zee and one day had almost elapsed. But I was still alive and still free.

As the girl had described, from the base of the old chimney I could see the round hill and the long-huts sprawling upon it. I swallowed some saliva. A hand instinctively felt the fire for reassurance. I had finally set myself apart.

Chapter 11

For the first time - even in the darkening light - I was able to see the markings at the end of the long-huts. On one was written WSW5 and had a phosphorescent glow - it was the place all right. I got closer and went up to its door. A warder (a guard) leant against the back of a chair outside. He was wrapped up against the evening chill, I couldn't tell if he had the disease or not. Or even if he showed its symptoms.

Emboldened by the action of the day I asked, 'I'm looking for some men.'

'Oh yeah,' he drawled.

'Ise gotten somethin' for em,' I quickly corrected my accent.

'Oh yeah?'

'Sure.'

'What youse got?'

'Somethin' on the hoof.'

'What youse mean?' He asked.

'I mean somethin' like you have inside, only this un walks.' (As if he didn't know.)

He eyed me suspiciously. 'Where's them other?'

'With im of course.' My accent seemed authentic enough – learnt from flics – new vocabulary added as I heard it.

The warder nodded towards the interior of the hut. I stepped in.

Inside I smelt again the burning wood from the stoves and the putrid air like heavy incense. The dark blinded me. But I saw the incandescent bodies in their neat rows. The glow from the fires. No sound. No movement. Until.

'Speak.'

'No names,' I said.

'Where's the business?'

'Come out of thems shadows,' I said, careful to keep my accent and not to speak like an Upper.

'Where's the business?'

'Where's the dob?'

'You'll get your credits soon enough.' Then from behind the light of the nearest stove an Upper showed his face. I could tell. But it was also the face of a snatcher.

'Pleased,' I said offering my hand.

He spat. I had made a slight mistake. I noticed his face twitch slightly.

'Where?'

'Outside. You alone?'

'What's it to you?'

'I need to know who I be trustin',' I answered.

Another figure stepped from the shadows.

'Bring him,' the first spoke. 'We need *real fresh*.'

'Sure,' I said, then, 'tell me, Ise curious, ain't done this afore, what happens to im?'

The two men looked at each other.

'I'm a new. Been sent to learn, understand? There be more...'

The two men exchanged glances.

'We take him back.'

'Back?'

'That's right. You're slow even for a sub, eh? You clean?'

'Aye,' I said. Then I asked, 'To Upper?'

'Where else?' the other spat, 'You think he's going to the Bridge?' They laughed. I pretended to be hurt. 'He's going to serve his government. This is no place for one of us, an Upper, now is it? Might catch something we don't want. Uppers are better than these "angles",' he laughed.

I realised then for certain that the subs who captured me knew I was an Upper. 'But youse have the shots,' I stated – as if I was no longer one of "them".

'Aye, and that's why *he's* in good condition, right? Right? He is in good, perfect, condition? He is an Upper? You ain't pulling a fast one?'

'Hese an Upper.'

'We don't pay top money for a sub. Subs can lie for awhile like these.'

'Nor a helper,' said the other. 'Don't need to hunt helpers.'

All the time I was speaking with them I was trying to think up a plan of action. They didn't appear armed but I knew they must have had weapons close by. Their attitude was casual and arrogant. I realised I was in a dangerous situation. But I felt like I was on a death wish anyway. I felt my luck had to run out sometime. I was sure my life was over.

'Lead the way sub.'

'Sure.'

We passed outside of the hut and down to its end. 'This is the way,' I said.

The two men followed obediently.

Recklessly I turned then and having taken out the pistol smashed it over the first's skull. I watched the violence of the metal split his skin and bruise the bone. His eyes whitened in the chilly air and he slumped down. The other froze in disbelief. I turned the gun quickly in my hand and rushed up to his face. With the barrel pointed at his forehead I said, 'Get down on the ground.' He did so. I looked back to see if the warder had seen anything, but as I thought he was hidden by the verandah posts.

'I'm going to kill you,' I said, 'unless you answer everything I ask, understand?'

'Yes.'

'If you're lucky, you'll get no more than your partner. Make a loud noise or a move and I'll blast you. Now, who are you?'

'Jen,' he spat.

'Who do you work for?'

'No one.'

I pushed the barrel into his face in the same manner I had done with the sub earlier.

'No one. We snatch. You know that. We snatch or we get given. There are subs who're always after a quick credit. These bleeding hearts would sell their own kin. Didn't you know?' (He knew by my accent, my actions that I was an Upper – maybe I was the one "on the hoof".)

'Where were you taking...' I went to say me. I looked into his eyes. Yes he knew all right. 'Where were you taking the body?' I pressed.

'Needed up. You know. We need perfection. Replacements. Fresh. You know.'

'I should kill you.'

'You need shots,' he said calmly. 'You ain't perfect. You're down.'

'What's it to you what I am?'

'What's it to *you*?' he reflected sternly.

'Don't need shots from scum like you.'

'You've got the disease. You're no use.'

'How do you know?' I said sharply.

'I can tell. Maybe we'd have cut you up quick enough to use. Maybe we'd have left you in one of the huts...'

I lifted the gun threateningly.

'Go on,' he jeered.

'What happens to those bastards?' I asked.

'We take them when needed. Not as good as a walking one, but they do. The subs swallow it. The subs know what's going on. It's a game. They talk about some dag religion. Some of the crazy subs walk into this hell. Holy-shell fuck. When we need limbs desperately we come for them - don't cost much, not as much as a live, fresh one. Reckon you haven't had the disease long,' he said slowly, 'reckon your mind's all right. Shame we didn't get you. A mind like yours would have been worth something...' he laughed. It took all my control not to kill him there and then.

'You working for the El?'

He shook his head.

'Don't you mess with me, you hear?'

He smiled.

'You working for the El?'

He smiled again. And so I smashed in his right eye ball. The scream from him, though I quickly smothered his face, was loud enough to warn the warder. I hit him again to knock him out. Sure enough the warder came. I hid. As he stepped towards the body I crunched him on the back of the skull. He went down heavily. I was getting crazed. I was losing all sense of morality. I was losing all sense of who I was. I felt as if I was disappearing.

Rushing back into the hut I pulled the pipes taking the blood mixture and thinning material to and from each of the beds. Was it my imagination or did I catch glimmers of thanks from those imprisoned bodies? Had I released them from the cruellest of oubliettes? Or had I just crawled into the deepest darkest hole myself?

Outside I took a quick breath and ran towards the scrub country. I cursed myself for not hunting for weapons but I knew time was against me; always against me. But tomorrow was another day. I thought back to the subs and how their blood would be thickening and clogging up their internal organs. How their minds might either be sent into a lasting frenzy or, I hoped, some peace before the final - and ultimate - stillness of death.

I wandered in the bleak countryside as the temperature dipped. From one of the hill tops I could look back and across to Wayland. It looked beautiful from a distance.

All I could do was try and find somewhere to spend the night as comfortably as possible. The thought of finding another hut crossed my mind - to lie in the fetid but warm air of the breathing zombies. But I also realised that if a police or army operated in subearth then all the huts would probably be investigated.

What I actually found out only half surprised me.

While I walked across the hill top I heard a buzzing sound from the distance. The sky was partially clear of cloud as the evening seemed to freeze. Scrambling down a bank I hid as two low-pulse helicopters approached. They travelled about a quarter of a league per minute and I was able to note everything about them. The markings showed they belonged to the inner government. And they were armed.

Down towards the valley floor there was a scooped piece of rock covered in part by a thick autumnal green bush (winter was only weeks away - the great solstice of Exmass). I crept in and huddled my body into a ball. The nutri-bars I had (wafers thinner than the bullets had also avoided detection) were quickly eaten but their energy staved off most of the effects of the cold - at least for some hours. It was as my body temperature dropped and the night grew blacker that I heard the terrible sounds of the night. I also became aware that my ankle had grown numb - the toe next to my big toe on my "good" foot was unnaturally cold also. I spoke out loud, 'The disease is tending.' And then I laughed; then I froze mentally. I had meant to say, 'spreading'. Was it the beginning of my mind breaking up? Or just the cold? Or just the effect of being apart from everything?

As I tried to take chunks of sleep all the images of my recent past came back to haunt me. There was the face of Zee emerging from the shadows when she first came to speak to me. There was the doctor probing me as I lay strapped to the table. My wife's face smiled from a sea of blank faces at some indistinguishable cocktail party. There was the face of the sub who had tried to sell me to the snatchers. The eyes of the sex-sub who had given me directions. The innocent face of baby Adam and the delight on the face of the woman who was to mother him. My world had collapsed. If I lived or died I did not care, but I was determined my wife and child should live.

It was true that I spent much of that cold lonely night thinking about my selfishness. But also about the emptiness of life in the Upper world. And I started to dwell on the name "mystery lands" which Zee had spoken of and wondered if these lands did indeed exist. I tried to put another plan together in my head. But each time I came up with something I would remember that I had the disease - and it was spreading. That without a shot I was doomed. And that I was no nearer sorting out Zee and the blackmailer. I was no nearer, indeed further, than when I had started.

Drifting in and out of consciousness, I found my dreams bleak and horrific. Once I woke from some snatched lifelessness to imagine a chimpanzee biting into the flesh of my calf. The irony was that I could not feel that calf. I got up and left the hiding place to stamp down the bank to the base of the valley. A stream ran at its bottom and reflected a briefly exposed glint of moonlight. It was eerie and beautiful. I splashed water onto my face. I wanted to drink from the stream, I had a terrible thirst, but I dared not risk it. So much of the water supply was contaminated. And I even laughed that I should care. I had the shellin' dag disease after all. I was no lucky holy-fuck.

I took out my final tube of dry water. Sucked on it. Then pissed into the stream. By that time I was far too cold to sleep again and so headed for the other side of the valley floor and the hill opposite. Walking set up a rhythm that seemed to keep me sane and warmer. I kept on getting the image of a chimp with the head of a human - a grotesque reality that bit into my sub-consciousness. I could not rid myself of the details of this aberration. And the face of Doctor Krenz would flood my mind with his smiling tiny-stumped teeth and cynical eyes.

Walking steadily I climbed the hill and then headed back towards Wayland. I had the chimney stack as a landmark, so I knew I could enter from a different direction. Stopping to examine the details from the digital of where Zee should be I glanced up at the sky and its developing bands of sunrise colour. The night had been long and drained me of much energy and boldness. In the distance there was a stone building, which I headed for.

Stars still shone away from the rising sun as I pushed a rotting wooden door open and dropped down onto a pile of stinking rags. As subearth grew warmer then sleep came upon me and curling into the foetal position I grabbed a couple of hours of much needed uninterrupted sleep.

A hole in the stone wall of the hut framed the sun that had climbed high enough to firstly bathe my face in its light, then irritate me into a yawning, sour-breathed yawn. It was Vendredi. I was still alone. But the power of the new day fortified me, and a resilience stirred once again.

At every opportunity I plotted positions and features into my digital. Risky enough. Taping the machine back against my skin I then took out the shiny paper of the map. I thought about how the map had been drawn; I realised how unused I was to reading (if not on a screen), writing or drawing. I tapped. I spoke. I ordered. But I rarely, if ever let my fingers hold a manual (pen/pencil). There was something deep in my thoughts that contemplated the freedom of this form of expression. Sure I could do anything with the digital but it dictated the parameters of expression. Maybe there was only a subtle difference in this range of expression compared with a manual but it intrigued me. I even stopped at one moment, took up a stone, and swished meaningless lines through some earthy dust. Only children did that kind of thing.

Back in Wayland I wrapped a cloth about my face (I had taken it from the stone hut), dropped my head down and walked stiffly in both legs. Nobody paid me a second glance. Most of the sex-subs ignored me, only the older ones or those with faces distorted by accidents and secondary diseases paid me attention. I thought about the Life Code. To exist; I did of sorts. To maintain the Laws; I had not. To credate; I had long ceased to. To increase; perhaps I already had. And...and? I had forgotten the last part of the code. I went through them all again, in different orders but I couldn't remember the last part. Or was it the first part? I panicked and broke out in a rush. The Code was part of every Upper's Nature. It was who we were and what distinguished us from the subs.

Stepping into the dark interior of a shop I felt for some money. I wasn't sure if the shop would take credit in the normal fashion. I wasn't sure if it would take money. I hung around until someone asked how much dob a piece of sorry-looking fruit was. 'Two thousand,' came the reply, 'or I'll take credit at 60%.' The customer laughed and then after a pause so did the shopkeeper. Looking in my pocket I found a five thousand. It was curious to handle this paper money (been difficult to get it legitimately). I needed to eat and drink something substantial. But I also had a terrible scratching pain inside my gut.

I still couldn't remember the final part of the Code. The shopkeeper asked me what I wanted and I bought some black bread and a clay pitcher of grog. As I handed over the dob I heard the buzz of low-pulses again. The shopkeeper took the dob suspiciously. The low-pulse grew loud enough for it to have landed. 'I need to shit,' I said. He half-smiled at the politeness of my expression, and realising my mistake, I said, 'I need to fuck-slurry.'

'Cost you.'

'Take it,' I said.

'Through the back on thems left.'

I moved stiffly to the back door in the blackness of shadow.

'Man,' he said, 'take this,' and he threw me a jar.

'Thankee.' The jar contained leaves. I shut the door behind me as an Upper pilot entered the shop. I didn't take the time to shit as I so desperately wanted but climbed out of the glass-less window and out into the back courtyard. I did empty the content of the pitcher before escaping. The jug I left by the slurry hole.

In another dark and damp corner I stuffed the bread into my mouth. Then I pissed standing and shitted squatting down. The leaves ran out. A child stuck his head round the corner and caught me. Paid no attention either. I was indistinct. And it was then that the final part of the Code came to me. Breathing deeply I convinced myself my mind was still in tact. But I was losing the sense of my own boundary. I was losing sense of the Life Code. Tightening my belt I kicked dust over the slurry and shuffled out into the narrow streets. I hung my head - but this time in a kind of shame.

Chapter 12

Carefully I looked at the map drawn on shiny paper. In darkened doorways or behind crumbling brick walls I scrutinized its shaky details as I got closer to where Zee was. The air was bright and cold and the sun slanted down its rays. My bones ached from the cold of the night before and I felt sluggish. The subs who pushed past both depressed and angered me. I should have felt pity but I only felt contempt.

No government soldiers or police were apparent as I turned down a littered close. At the end of this was the gate with the symbol noted on the map. The symbol was a bell superimposed upon a three-leafed plant. The door opened creakily and I stepped into a yard. It might only have been my imagination that rats scuttled between discarded bricks and bags of rubbish.

A doorway with a green canopy faced me. I went up to it and banged hard. Nothing happened. I slammed my fist against the peeling paint of the door's wood. And waited. After about five minutes the door was finally opened. A child looked up at me.

'What youse want?' the child asked.

I looked down at her dirty but pretty face. 'Want speak I to Zee.'

The child quickly went to heave the door to, but I caught my foot between it and the door jamb. Rather roughly pushing the girl to one side I went into the gloom.

A man approached me from the shadows. 'Who be yer?'

'I'm looking for Zee,' I said calmly.

'No Zee,' he said and raised his arm. Taking the pistol from my trouser pocket I waved it at him. 'She'll know I,' I said.

'Who?'

'Adam.'

'Adam?' he repeated.

'Yes. Adam X.'

Zee had been in the doorway of a room off the dark corridor. 'Adam,' she smiled coming up to me and nodding at the sub thug. 'Good to see thee.'

'I'm sure.'

'Fetch some grog,' she said to the thug. 'Come, follow me...'

She led me through into a room, which, though shadowy, was not unpleasant.

'How did you find me?' She used her usual diction of an Upper. She did a good job of not seeming that surprised to see me. Perhaps word had spread.

'I had help,' I said curtly.

'What do you want?' she said directly, matter-of-factly.

'Answers.'

'Haven't I given you answers,' she said.

'Not enough.'

'Sit,' she said.

I looked at her beautiful face with disdain, yet there was still something about her...

'I heard about you,' she said.

'Really?'

'News travels.'

'Especially when you have a government informer...'

'Helpers too,' she smiled. 'I didn't want things to turn out as they have, you know that. I've only ever wanted to get my child to your world...to safety.'

'And yourself.'

'Maybe,' she said. 'You don't know anything. You've had it bad. I didn't want that. Things have got out of hand.'

'What are you doing here, now? Where is he?'

'You still don't know? Still don't know who he is?'

I shook my head and smiled facetiously. A glint of sunlight tried to find itself into the room. She began to prepare a fire in the grate. The thug came in with grog - it was hot and spicy.

'Just like the rest of you,' I said, sweeping my arm about, 'I got, get information from helpers, at the right price. That's all it takes isn't it? Credits. Dob. Favours - you know. The holy-fuck shell. Or government electronic papers.' I let the last sentence hang.

'Go ahead,' she said, 'let it out, why shouldn't you?'

'You're all shellin' scum,' I spat.

'What do you know? Now you've got the disease, now you're an outcast, think you have all the answers - right?'

'Haven't I?'

'The shell you have.'

'Then tell me.'

'I was stuck in this place. Stuck in subearth. I didn't have the disease. You'd think that would be good, eh? I mean, what could be worse than having the disease? But my life and my family's were made an oubliette because I was clean and pure-limbed. The diseased hated me, spat at me and tried to infect me (as if they could). The holy-pimps wanted to make money out of me since I reached eleven years old. The snatchers wanted to zombie me and slice my body up for a shellin' Upper. The family was shunned - like all those with some pure in them. And I couldn't get enough money for a helper interview. But yes, I didn't have the disease. What the dag eh?'

I listened. All the while she talked she made the fire, crouching before the grate and turning her head round to me. She continued:

'He came down to do business. For dob. For credit. Just like us. Just like us filthy subs, eh?' The fire crackled into life. The grog was making me feel sleepy and I longed for heat.

'He took a fancy to me - like you took a fancy to me. That's the way it goes, right? Promised me things. Took risks for me. Took me to Upper and kept me secret. Maybe he kept me a prisoner. But hey, I ate well. I had helpers for servants. If I didn't see daylight, well, I was used to it. He treated me well. Said he was going to get me "papers". But he needed credit. And then I got pregnant. And that confused things.' She placed stronger pieces of wood onto the fire. The flames licked up and cast waving shadows across the walls.

'I gave him my body and soul. I gave him everything. I fell in love. We fall in love in subearth you know. We have feelings. But I had to come back here to have the baby. To this house. This mission. The Bell Sisters. They looked after me. They would have brought me up too. Away from the slurry of the gossiping subs. Looked after the baby until my mother could smooth things at the house. But he didn't abandon me you see. He got me e-papers (an electronic coded pass) to be a helper. And he knew you. He knows you. Got me work with you. And you fell for everything. Just because a helper had a pretty face...'

'Not just,' I said.

'Maybe...But you played along. And our plans seemed to go so well. But...'

'But?'

'You know. *You* are what went wrong. He got greedy. Wanted more. Needed more dob; needed to get me shots and clearance and a way to get the boy back. A boy I haven't seen since you handed him over to that slurry-cow.'

'It's what you wanted,' I protested.

'Nothing is what I wanted,' she declaimed. 'But it was the best I could do. And now, now he's gone too far, and here you are, staring me in the face like guilt manifest.'

'I am ruined,' I stressed.

'Yes.'

'What do I do?'

She fell silent. Turned to the fire and stoked it.

After some time with the fire healthy and emitting waves of warmth she began to speak again. 'He's coming here tomorrow.'

'Him?'

'Yes, I'm sure you knew…'

I said nothing. Then after a moment, 'So, he's meeting you here?' I wanted confirmation.

'Yes. To give me shots and to tell me if he has found a way to squeeze dob from your wife.'

'My wife? Hasn't she suffered enough?'

'She'll be protected by the Commander. You know that...'

'I don't know. It isn't fair. I came down here to get money *back*. To get shots myself. To return in time for no-one to know...'

'Too late,' she smiled. 'You know it's too late. You're kind of a hero at the moment. Except they'd all kill you if they could. You're worth something.'

I caught a glint in her eye. 'And does that mean you'll sell me too?'

'No,' she said. 'I can't...I can't...' she stood up and before me. 'All I want is for my child to be safe. He's going too far, he's going to expose the identity of the child - I'm sure. The Eloluc know about you and they must know about him. The Eloluc have hired a catcher. *The Catcher.*'

I strained my eyes in disbelief.

'They want all this done away with. No corruption on the Register. No corruption in Records. Though you're both minor players they can see a chain growing.'

'What's to be done?' I asked looking across at her heart-shaped face.

'He comes tomorrow. I will tell you this – if you don't know. He comes here at the end of the third quarter and...You must do what is right. For myself, I don't care. All I ask is for the child to be kept secret and brought up in privilege.'

'Even in the world you despise?'

'I despise them both. Both worlds. What options have I?'

'Tell me Zee,' I said eventually. 'You talked of the "mystery lands". Do they truly exist?'

'Yes.'

'How do you know?'

'Because I *know*,' she said.

I looked long and hard at her.

'There is much you don't know.'

'Whatever might happen to me,' I said, 'could you help my wife to escape there.'

'Does she need to escape?'

'You know she does.'

Again she paused for a long time. 'I will try.'

'Couldn't you have escaped there – all the subs and your children?'

Zee laughed enigmatically.

'Tell me something else Zee,' I urged.

'Go ahead.'

'Weren't, aren't, you afraid of catching the disease from me?'

'You think I care after all these years? Don't you think I would have caught the disease by now?'

'I...'

'Maybe your scientists should do some research on the likes of me rather than trying to hunt us down like vermin.'

The weather had changed. The fire had calmed down. The grog had warmed me from the inside.

'You can't stay here,' she said.

'I know.'

'It's the way it is, the Sisters don't approve of men - only those who protect us...'

'Can I sleep for an hour or so?' I asked.

'Yes,' she said kindly. 'I want it all settled,' she said wearily, 'I want it all settled and I want to see change; is that a paradox?'

I listened to the way she spoke. How different she seemed from the other subs.

'You speak well,' I said.

'Oh, aye. Speak I likes unt good Upper, yeah?'

'I don't mean to be patronising.'

'Well you are,' she added with her usual zeal.

'Do you, do you have schools?' I asked timidly.

'There are some. I was lucky. Near the border - to the south - there are pick-up points for your computer schools. I was chosen. I've knowledge enough. How else could I have made it as a helper without the indoctrination? And I can still sniff out crawlies...'

'And *raths* - beasties?' I remembered her fear in the house.

'Maybe.'

'It's all wrong,' I half said to myself.

'Oh, yese waking up,' she laughed, 'I thought you wanted to sleep.' Her words rang out not unkindly. She carried on, 'We have a government here. It's corrupt, it will do anything to ingratiate itself with you Uppers and it has little money or power...we have rebels too. You didn't know? There's some. Some exist close to the mystery lands, so they say,' she half-laughed. 'And we have places for people to get patched up - or cut up as spare parts,' she looked at me fiercely, 'and there are those who clean up the pure...'

'Pure?'

'Not the able-bodied. No. Shit, fuck-slurry' she smiled. 'And occasionally they do something about the rubbish. But then again when everyone is dying from within the body or the brain, who cares about shit?'

I looked into my mug of grog. 'Quite,' was all I could say.

'Have you heard those poor bastards who have lost their minds, the screamin' people? Can't put a coherent sentence together - hey what's the point of educating them? Just for them to go shellin' nuts,' and she laughed, 'a few years after? Some of those bastard mad people are really crazy. *Really* crazy,' she said.

'Can't they be helped?'

'Can't the disease be helped?'

'Can't anything be done?'

'Dear bleeding heart, you're a slurry-government worker aren't you?'

'I was.'

'There's no hope for us,' she continued, 'no hope without shots. That's why we do what we do. Anything to get clean - pure,' again she laughed, 'in the conventional sense,' she added. 'And the lucky ones, like me, get to have an education and to know exactly what it is to have nothing.'

I drained the grog from the mug. There was nothing cosy left inside me. My thoughts ran compulsively back to my wife.

'Stay for awhile,' she said suddenly. 'You are a good man, I'm sure of it. I wanted you to change something in your world. Now you are without a world, as am I. Perhaps things will change when you meet. Him.'

'Can you tell me his name?'

'Be patient.' Her mood darkened. 'How I would love to know the life of an Upper woman. How I would love to know the life of my child. The first of his kind, perhaps. Perhaps a new man, Adam – Adam X.?'

She called me by my name and it sounded sweet. Rested sweetly upon me.

'You remember your first visit to subearth?' she asked.

'Yes.' For how could I forget?

'They called you the angel...remember?'

'Something like that,' I said.

'They believe the angel of darkness will lead them to the Bridge. And across the Bridge will lie their heaven. Their White Rooms,' she laughed.

'You know?'

'I know.'

'And they thought I was the angel?'

'Maybe you are,' she said. 'Maybe you can lead them all across the Bridge and into the great abyss at its other end.'

'Why are you saying this?' I asked.

'Because...because I feel it,' she added.

I was curious but I asked no more.

'Stay,' she said, 'until the beginning of the fourth quarter, then the Sisters will be back from their work. Then you will have to slip out and into the darkening night. This is all I can do - until tomorrow.'

'Thank you,' I said.

She smiled. Walked towards me, dropped down on her haunches and kissed me lightly. 'Thank you,' she said.

Chapter 13

I slipped out from the Bell Sisters' mission house a different way than I had entered. Zee had given me some food and a worn jacket to wear - one she thought would help me blend even better into subearth. She also gave me an address where I could spend the last quarter of the day and the opening quarter of Samedi.

Outside rain lashed down and I soon heartily missed the fire and grog of the mission. Zee had told me that the Sisters could be seen in the streets of subearth, recognisable by their ringing of a tiny bell. Those girls who needed help could approach a Sister and would be given a miniature bell-clapper as a pass. Girls as young as seven had been preyed on for sex in the harsh alleyways of subearth. Girls as young as ten and eleven had fallen pregnant. Any pregnancy was keenly watched over in subearth.

The rain fell on dirty streets. Washing I had seen hung between buildings had mostly been gathered in. The rain emphasised the great desperation of the people. But still children played out of doors in puddles, which were growing into lakes. I saw older men drunk on grog and vomiting into the streams of filthy water that rushed alongside crumbling curbs. I wondered if Wayland had once been a town like those in Upper - clean-angled with flashing lights adorning crisp-leafed trees.

Nobody stopped me as I bent my head against the driving and piercing shafts of rain. Nobody accused me of being the angel. Men and women hung themselves in doorways or crammed their ragged bodies about dampened braziers. Occasionally mules, sometimes horses, or *very rarely* trucks would transport piles of wood. I saw one such truck (though not laden with wood) stop outside a shop and disgorge a great pile of tins. There was an economy of sorts, I gathered. How people made their money seemed unfathomable. I knew credit came from Upper; I knew everyone in subearth was entitled to enough to survive – or rather subsist. Whatever they could make on top of those payouts was theirs to keep.

Rats thrived as rainwater gathered in the dips of roadways. Rubbish floated and effluent - shell-slurry - made the stink of the place worse. I didn't realise how low a man, a man like me, could sink. I was wet through and cold. Some buildings had the lights of candles or gas lamps but most only cast shadows of fires (some government buildings were supposed to have electricity). Braziers spat red ash into the oppressive sky.

Every now and then I would feel for the digital taped against my body. It was my record. I tapped in co-ordinates from time to time. Information from the sky was not as forthcoming in subearth so I had to make mental notes of where I had been. It was hardly necessary - the place burnt itself into my consciousness. I knew I could be tracked too – but that would take a little time.

Even with the rain and the dark descending I witnessed subs with their chilled and diseased flesh ravaged by bites from rats. I could see torn flesh un-bleeding. I saw accidents barely registered by a cry or a scream. I heard the mumbo-jumbo of the deranged. Unintelligible language gushing from spittle-flecked lips or mouths locked exaggeratedly tight. Sometimes I would see bodies of highlighted perfection. Were these Uppers (and what were they doing?) or those such as Zee? I also saw directions to fights and scar-faced men keeping watch out. By one of these fight buildings I saw a mule-drawn wagon arrive and holy-stoners alight awkwardly out of its back. Naked, white, chalky flesh - somehow even worse than the destitute life of those grimly thriving, surviving, in Wayland.

On reaching the address Zee had given me I looked to my right and left. I had finally disappeared; become invisible. I had been gone from the Upper world for two days and yet it felt like a lifetime. The house in front of me was separated from its neighbours; was in the same kind of run down condition but hidden to some extent by bushes and twisted-branched trees. I went to its side and found a way round the back - as Zee had explained. In an area of stone-flagging a group of subs drank grog around a fire. The rain hissed as it landed on the burning wood and hot ashes. They seemed not to notice me as I dropped down into a stone culvert about five-feet deep. There, as Zee had promised, was an opening into the building. The smell of damp and slurry knocked me back. The blackness of the place was terrifying.

Taking the night-light and matches (that Zee had wrapped up) I struck a match against a wall. The initial brightness of light brought the walls of the place shockingly close and eerily real. The wick shivered into life and light and settled the shadows slowly. The room I was in was small. Scuttling creatures brought piles of rag and paper to life. There was graffiti on the walls. "Free Pandlam" shone luminously.

It was up to me to find a safe place to rest. I headed for the door at the far end of the room and reached it almost solely through following the smell of concentrated ammonia. Occasionally I stopped to listen for movement. I imagined crawlies scooting along the dirty walls. I imagined rats having enough boldness to attack me. But I also prayed to god that they would sense my still - comparatively - vigorous health - though I had limped upon my right foot enough to keep me safe in the streets. (I did not know if the disease was spreading or if lack of sleep and the weather worsened it - I had last looked at the cut in my big toe four days before. The sight of that dry gash sickened me. The previous night I had felt the plaster and bandage weaken as I walked across the valleys and over the hilltops of subearth.)

The light I carried became dimmer and yet its effect somehow greater. The area illuminated was some holy-dag greatness. It was holy-dag to me. I reached the bottom of a flight of stairs and had to make a decision whether or not to climb or find a room on the same level. Not wishing to use the other night-light, I had to think and act fast. I decided to climb. Rain played on the outer walls and roof of that strangely abandoned building, but there was a deathly quiet within it too. I recalled the imagery of the oubliette; being buried alive; rotting alive. I felt a drop of water land on my face and imagined the drop of a crawlie's body with its disgusting brown legs creeping over my flesh. But it could never add to my disease.

The stairs creaked under each of my movements. The wood gave and I worried that each step's rottenness would break under my weight. Rising up into the blackness only added to my forbearing, but climbing gave me a drop of courage also. Courage dripped into an ocean of fear. It was the sense that anything seemed possible in the hell-hole of subearth.

The landing stretched into a black void. With some light cast I saw that doors led off to my right and left and also another staircase rose to a higher level. The surrounding dark was oppressive. The dark created the light and life of my imagination. With the dim glow of the night-light and my increased imagination I was actually able to throw dim images against the black back-drop. The sound of rain had died down. Drips could be heard somewhere distant in that old decaying building. The night-light was beginning to twitch into nothingness. I decided to investigate farther down the corridor but not to climb the stairs. As I brought round the flame and with it the chasing shadows I heard a banging in the "somewhere" below. I almost dropped the light with fright.

Where a front door might have given onto the road I heard the sound of thumping, and, I thought, the sound of raised voices. Quickly I walked down the corridor into the gloom of my raised light. Darkness was closing in and the light's glow was penetrating less. There was a door to my right that I pushed open as more banging echoed through the house. Once inside this room I shut the door fast and turned round abruptly. The night-light was extinguished by my sudden movement. The blackness seemed to rush into my throat and stifle the breath of courage from me. My heart raced and sweat formed upon sweat (even though the night was cold).

Fumbling for a match I dropped the used night-light and unwrapping the spare held it in my left hand. With my right I struck the match on the face of the wall. I thought I heard a noise. Felt my bowels loosen. Tasted grog in my throat. The ignited light gave reassurance. There was no-one in there. The room was high-ceilinged, had an old fire-place and was quite long. I spent some time searching its corners and decided to try and burn the debris in the grate. There was only the smell of damp and I was thankful no holy-fuck sub had slurried.

Smoke rising out of the chimney would be lost into the choked air of Wayland, I figured. There were still a few drops of rain spitting down into the fireplace so at least the chimney wasn't blocked. I only had a few matches to play with but some of the wood I found was rotten and dry. Occasionally I listened out for noises down below - or the creak of stairs. And as I rummaged through the room's debris I was conscious of the creepies and crawlies or the blooded bodies of rats.

When the fire had developed into a strong blaze I relaxed slightly; blew out the night-light and placed it on the mantelpiece. The windows in the room had been boarded up and I thought about prising the wood off for the fire when the night was at its heart. There was enough stuff to burn for a while. Smoke blew back from the chimney and made me cough. In the strange light of the fire I rested up close to its heat and took off my boots and socks. I examined my big toe. It still had no feeling. The bandage I was able to wrap around well enough but the plaster and lint I threw onto the flames.

For some time I contented myself with gazing into the fire or searching out more things to burn but eventually I became very aware of where I was and the darkness surrounding the edge of my vision. Beyond the limit of concrete perception I saw the demons of the sub-conscious. I also got the nagging constant worry that I was not alone in the house. That I was trapped where I was. That there was nowhere to run. It was an oubliette. Also a quietness seemed to exist beyond the range of the fire's weird noises. Part of me wanted to go from the room and search the whole damn place - part of me was so terrified that it wished only to remain frozen to the spot.

In order to distract the growing wildness of my fear I tried to think about what would happen the next day. Tried to imagine who it was who could have betrayed me. Tried to remain brave for the sake of my wife - I had much to put right. But each time the fire burnt down the more I grew petrified.

In the jacket Zee had given me I found food. Not much, but a little something to chew on; there was also a capsule. Undoing the cap of this I tapped out a couple of pills. Without too much thought I knocked them back; I didn't care what their effect might be. Nothing was worse than the thought of utter darkness. The idea I could be incarcerated into an oubliette. And with only the oubliette of oblivion as a form of escape. The pills took time to be swallowed. I waited. Listened. Sweated. And before long I was fast asleep.

It was a loud sound either in my dreams or in reality that woke me up. But even now I don't know if what I experienced then belonged to the real world or its flip side of nightmare. As I awoke I opened my eyes wide then shut them quickly. Slowly consciousness returned as I heard the spitting of the fire. Dying flames curled around one of the last remaining pieces of salvaged wood. I remember shuddering with cold and opening my eyes tentatively becoming aware of the darkness closing in on me. But then I became aware of something else too.

There was the feeling that I was not alone in the room. I felt the hairs on the back of my neck rise and an unbearable lightness overwhelm my body. Without understanding fully why, I peered into the core of the blackness. There seemed to be speckled lights, which I took to be the fault of my vision. My ears were "pinned back" ready to intercept the slightest movement and its sound. But the room and house were deadly quiet.

After freezing my vision for some time, a time that seemed eternal, I thought I saw something growing in the deepest darkest corner of the room. And there was a sound that hummed inside my head but which I could not identify. In the corner I began to see a paleness - a gloominess coalesce. I was utterly transfixed. The sound in my head grew and blocked out some of my rationality. The paleness grew into the shifting features of a face. And the face grew eyes that penetrated the darkness so that they appeared closer to me than their surrounding ghostly skin. I felt pinned down by these eyes. The eyes looked deep inside me and seemed to merge with the humming noise that washed across my mind flooding myriad frightened thoughts.

Still absolutely frozen to the spot I witnessed the face grow into a lightness that formed the basic shape of a figure. The eyes, which had appeared in front of me, now hovered right before my own; sucked me into their swirling pupils that shone dark and deathly blue - though their colour was hard to determine. The body of this thing waved about the periphery of my vision like miasma. It was as if nothing existed in the entire world but my inner self; the terrible humming sound (buzzing and tormenting my mind) and the staring eyes. And then everything became black again.

And it seemed at that moment that I had woken for the first time and the sight of the unearthly body was only the tail end of a terrible nightmare. But it felt real and remained with me mentally and physically. I actually felt sick. Felt cold and shivery. It was as if something from another time and place had looked deep inside me. I could not move. Only as the fire lost all its light did I stand with great speed - as if unlocked from a spell - and fumbling take the night-light from the mantelpiece. With difficulty and some panic I lit this and held its flame aloft. And yet again I sensed the rushing in of darkness and the great divide between myself and everything else. And I also thought about the baby in my wife's womb. And I saw clearly Zee's face closing in upon my own.

I walked over to the door but could not look into the shadow where the apparition had been, opened the door with trembling hand and felt the coldness of the corridor stroke my face. Rain thundered on a roof somewhere; there was a tremendous smell of damp. I heard some banging too, but there was a wind blowing through the building then that threatened to extinguish my light. I reached the top of the stairs and looked down to another source of light that bathed a hallway. And I thought I saw movement across this silvery illumination; the fleeting shape of a luminous figure. I wanted to shout out. Inside my mind complete quiet had taken hold, as if most of my mind was frozen. I ran down the stairs, hardly touching the rotten wood. Hardly conscious of my movement.

In the room where I had entered originally I witnessed again the graffiti, it read: 'Free Subearth'. Was that what I had seen originally? I wasn't so sure. From the window where I had climbed in I could see light reflected against the wall opposite. Rain had ceased. With terror induced haste I got myself out and hauled myself up into the garden and yard of the empty building. The subs had disappeared but their fire still burnt. The wind had stilled as suddenly as it had risen. One side of the sky twinkled with stars and the moon shone but in the distance a glow signalled the coming dawn. Rain clouds had been chased into the distance. It was Samedi arriving. I caught deep breaths, looked back at where I had come from. Looked up at the boarded windows of a room where I might have been and...And I thought I saw the vague outline of a figure peering down at me.

Pushing away the touch of leaves and bare branches I made my way to the road. Life groaned on. A kind of semi-life. Had Zee known something about that place? I spat on the floor. Smelt the sulphur in the air. Heard a distant cry. Saw two subs arm in arm - full on grog. And I concentrated on a face. A face out of nowhere. But the face was half familiar. And the face came from a different world. From Records. From the Register. From the Blackmailer?

Hate tore into me. Hate shook away the fear inside of me. I was ready to challenge everything. Even ghosts from the past.

Chapter 14

At a pre-determined point The Catcher ditched his car and uncovered the hover bike. Everything went to plan. After placing the box containing the beastie into a pannier and sheathing the rifle, he sped off. The bike rolled across the pitted track or lifted above the ground when serious hazards approached. The Catcher's steely eyes stared into the distance. He carried the Eloluc motif on the gleaming metal of the bike and his digital bore all the information he might require.

On the roads and tracks of subearth the bike effortlessly lifted its bulk and glided noiselessly. The machine took cuts across the barren countryside and purred out its power. The destination was one of the long-huts.

It was a glorious Samedi morning with the weather bright and chilly. The winds of Vendredi night had blown away the rain clouds and the sun had risen and shone weakly over su and Upper alike. The Catcher thought about indulging in some white-bodying while he was in subearth. The thought of accruing more credit lifted his spirits. The idea that he would eradicate a transgressor - a government transgressor at that - raised his spirits still further. The usual method of paralysing a victim (the zombiefication as it was known colloquially) and then bringing him back to Upper was not to be. The Catcher drew no emotional delight from witnessing either the interrogation of a criminal or the slow dismembering and mind-suck.

The Catcher enjoyed working with the *raths* and beasties (which the *raths* became); enjoyed the relationship he developed with each one. The beastie he carried with him had proved quite a challenge in fact. For some time it had not responded to his "whispering"; had not responded to the messages from his DNA. But The Catcher thrived on this challenge. Life was too easy for him. And he had relished the need to modify some of the beasties non-organic matter.

The Eloluc still asked for his advice when they developed their military insects. It was he that had pioneered the insertion of robotic parts; the ability of insects to be tracked and monitored and for them to be used as incendiary devices. A swarm of wasps or bees fitted with minute nuclear devices or packed with diseases (other than *the* disease) could or would wreak havoc. But that was all work of his youth. For many years he had lived the life of a hermit, communicating only with the spiders; learning how to "whisper" to them; learning how to direct and control them; learning how to track down transgressors with these creatures; learning the ways to zombiefy or eradicate. And The Catcher had trained many others too. But he was only truly content holding a beastie upon the palm of his hand blowing soft breath across it - or working in the laboratory to convert an organic crawlie into a deadly *hunter-rath*.

The Catcher headed for hut SWS4. The long-hut was on his way to the extermination. He had business with snatchers there. One of the Eloluc needed fresh parts for an ageing family member; The Catcher knew exactly who scratched his back in Upper. Arranging body parts for an Eloluc was necessary if he wanted to call in favours later. He cruised on over the scrubby hills of that part of subearth. He felt neither disdain nor compassion for the people who lived there. He cared little for any non-*rath* being and especially despised the subs weaknesses.

At SWS4 he was able to park the bike and know that the warder would take care of it. All the warders and guards of the long-huts were in the pay of the Upper government. Each of the subs they kept alive with a kind of grim and mock reverence was destined for eventual use by Uppers. The warders were actively encouraged to procure young subs and halt the spread of their disease with drugs given by the (Upper) government (there was a tacit agreement that the warders would get this drug too - a kind of shot – and there was a sometime illegal trade in the substance. Some subs believing "weedle" was derived from it). This sate of affairs had either the tacit or occasionally explicit encouragement by su's puppet government. The drugs given to the "lucky ones" would still give the impression they had the disease (their minds were locked and they could be "sniffed") but suspending it in a way that kept their near or actually perfect young bodies in a kind of *stasis* – or suspended animation. It worked very well. No questions needed to be asked. The subs thought this "form" of the disease simply a quirk and that its sufferers were indeed "lucky" - though they were happy these "lucky ones" were out of sight and mind (however deranged).

"Perfect" subs would be enticed by an elaborate mis-description of "life" in the long-huts. It was said to be part of the Bridge – and a mythology had grown around this. They were fledgling angels. It was a kind of bizarre suicide-cult without immediate death. It was considered a way to avoid the squalor of life in subearth. To rest peacefully and pure. Others didn't come voluntarily.

There was therefore, thanks to these "angles", a healthy trade in fresh limbs but *this* was kept as covert as possible. Most of subearth went along with the "culture", "spirituality" of the "near-dead". Everyone seemed to accept that the bodies would eventually be "dissolved" (or "processed" – "crossing the Bridge") in the usual manner so that the disease would spread no further. If the folk of su were forced to think about those in the long-huts it was with dismissive pity or feigned reverence – most simply chose not to think. Someone else was taking care of these subs - preserving their bodies until ultimate death – and no rats would chew them up. Perhaps some (especially those working for the su government) had more than an inkling of what was going on – but as long as they were safe, "angelic", who knows perhaps even disease-free, they kept quiet. It was better to keep quiet. Especially if you were disease free. What might happen if you spoke out? In this way the people of subearth were no different to the collective and selective amnesiacs of Upper.

But the long-huts with their procured subs could not meet the demand from Upper. That is why the body-snatchers worked in hit squads in su. Able-bodied subs lived in fear of many things and being snatched was only one. Snatchers were only too aware of course of what was happening – more so than lowly government officials. And even when a person was snatched on the street - "disappeared" - people tended to keep their mouths shut and not ask questions. Life was hard enough. Life was a struggle. There was always the disease to worry about. The only thing a disease-free, able-bodied sub could truly hope for was to be chosen as a helper. Many subs arrived in Upper illegally to become helpers. Those who made it would send back credit – those who didn't (those not pure enough) would never be heard of again. Maybe spent the rest of their lives lying unknown in a long-hut. Angels in transience.

The Catcher thought it only reasonable that the "clean" brains and minds of subs be used for the extension of the lives of the Uppers; the Eloluc in particular. The use of body parts he never even questioned. One day he would need one of those parts. The Uppers had developed amazingly responsive artificial limbs but there was a prejudice towards organic. And, indeed, the organic grafts proved very successful. Aged Uppers had taken healthy limbs and quickly colonised them; had taken internal organs and quickly infused them with their own blood. Screening took time of course. But a sub's healthy body indicated - if not lack of disease - then the ability to hold the disease at bay. And limbs from the bodies in the long-huts could be used, the disease cleaned out and isolated. And being in the long-huts acted as a kind of quarantine – healthy (though apparently life-less) subs were obviously more expensive and chosen first. "On the hoof", fresh, disease-free subs were best. Straight from sub hell to Upper heaven – no "limbo" for them.

There had been great debates amongst those in the inner government about the use of children for body parts; but again the question of the disease's ability to remain undetected in a child's body had meant not - thus far. Many of the barren women of Upper had clamoured for adoption rights (based on lengthy quarantine) and for the use of spare parts from the children for their damaged own. But the laws remained unchanged. Many of the Upper parents argued it would be reasonable for mind swaps between imbecile Upper children and sub children destined for the White Rooms. That, however, was considered immoral.

The Catcher met the warden and was taken through the hut, past the rows of beds and the suffocating air to the back office. It was here that the bodies were processed. According to the laws the subs had to have "died" by then, in fact it was usual for them to be transported "on the hoof" though not of course "fresh". In the back room with a gas lamp burning and a fire in a grate flaming (unlike the choking stoves in the main room) The Catcher talked business with a couple of surly-looking snatchers. He knew about the incident at WSW5 but dismissed their idea that it was rebel action.

The Catcher had been given an order for an Eloluc whose wife needed a fresh set of eyes. The snatchers suggested a live catch but The Catcher was content to first walk amongst the subs and see for himself. In each hut there were about fifty subs held at any one time. Most were young. Some had been given up by their own families when they reached a certain age (alas credit could be obtained). Given up as *angles linking hands on the Bridge.*

At a young age the "perfect" subs could easily become the targets of jealous and vengeful diseased subs. Could be harmed and given the disease – so relatives might argue. Unless they were considered to be of the quality for future helpers (which suggested at least a rudimentary education or reasonable level of intelligence) the hapless bodies of the perfect (or sometimes near-perfect) could indeed be attacked, stolen or deliberately mutilated. Families sometimes acted ruthlessly with their own – what was the sacrifice of one son or daughter if the credit they received meant a better life for the rest? And so the idea blossomed that a family was *blessed* by having a relative in a long-hut and the credit given by the warders, meant a steady, if insufficient stream. Better to have credit than a mutilated, helpless mouth to feed. Families could boast of an "angel" whose very "wings" supported them. Perhaps it was simple cruelty. Perhaps they believed truly in the Bridge. In the angels of the long-huts. Of Lord Satan and the dark one. Perhaps they believed what they needed to. And the need for and acquisition of credit brutalised their lives

The Catcher strode between the rows of beds. If a sub took his eye he would saunter over and gaze into their "terrified" eyes; or rather their passive eyes. And one of the subs, a young woman with perfect white skin, did take The Catcher's attention. He glared down upon her. Touched her face, feeling its coldness. Examined the lids of her eyes. 'She will do,' he said. And the warder tapped in her number. She would be taken "on the hoof" to Upper and her eyes plucked from her face. The rest of her body would be dismantled, though at so short notice it would be unlikely her mind would be required. Her brain could be used for experimentation and research. The Catcher was expert enough – he had intended fresh eyes – but hers were very good.

The Catcher found it both macabre and amusing to pull back the sheet from the subs and run a hand over their dry-feeling bodies. He found it interesting and stimulating to think about their intelligence, which (probably) still registered his authority. And he always admired the ability of the Upper doctors to test those who had or didn't have the disease; and to distinguish amongst the diseased those whose minds hadn't been eaten away. He stopped and thought. Out of the hut he was currently in, probably only sixty percent were totally unaware of their horrific fate and certainly another twenty percent knew exactly what was happening to them - or rather not happening to them. For the *sense of protocol* meant they might be kept for years in that paralytic state. A sham, he thought, an utterly pointless sham. No Bridge for the. No bliss-infused stasis. Only static hell.

He fancied that the sub whose eyes stared upwards before him then was one who understood what was going on. It was a gift The Catcher supposed he had. Sometimes he would even get a sub taken from the long-huts and treated in the necessary fashion to become a white-bodier; to be a personal fighter for him...to be used for up to three fights, if all were won of course. But the eyes that stared up belonged to a beautiful young girl. Her eyes were not the equal of the young woman's he had already chosen (and perhaps not quite big enough) but...there was something about them and her. The Catcher shooed the warder and snatchers away.

The air of the place almost choked him. He hated the tubes leading to the chalk bodies. But the girl's eyes intrigued him. Pulling back the thin sheet he revealed her young body, breasts standing upright, not falling to her sides. Her flat stomach and rise of her pudenda. The Catcher aimlessly stroked her body and watched for movement or a flicker from her eyes. There seemed nothing and yet there seemed something. He put his face down close to hers.

'You will die in pieces,' he spoke softly. 'I want you to know. Your terror isn't over. Think about this. Fill your time with this thought.'

Again he scrutinised her eyes. Should he use the eyes of this girl? But the young woman's were a better match. Perhaps he was wrong this time. But he was The Catcher and he was seldom, no, *never* wrong. And he wanted to think about the young girl lying for months to come inwardly tortured by the thoughts of her eventual fate.

The Catcher knew the kind of sordid business that went on in the long-huts. It was the prerogative of the warders to holy-fuck the bodies. Some had caught the disease that way, even though sheathed (for the bodies were diseased and disease-free alike – only their "perfect" limbs connected them). Some who were snatched seemed to be disease-free and there was no way of telling when the body appeared perfect. In their bodily stasis there must have been many who slowly lost their minds - not just from the imposed paralysis but from the disease itself. And there were plenty of sadistic warders who found other ways to amuse themselves. But the penalty for defacing a sub in a long-hut was to join them. And nobody but other warders would ever know. Old scores could be settled with a false denunciation. The Catcher laughed.

At the front porch the men laughed and joked. The warder disappeared occasionally to stoke the stoves and keep their fires burning. Smoke billowed from the chimney. The day almost warmed up. The Catcher held his hand in his pocket. He had begun the tickling. Yes the beastie was a difficult one. But he began to "whisper" to it through his skin. The beastie moved silently over the palm of his hand but was kept captive in that palm. The whisper told it of an Upper who had transgressed, who worked on the Register, who worked for the Records and who was not to be zombiefied but was to be *eradicated*.

The Catcher felt the movements of the spider. He maintained a conversation of sorts with the snatchers and even talked with the warder - a sub. But all the while he felt the sweat form on his hand and felt the connection with the legs of the *rath*. Felt the exchange of communication between their DNA. Felt the buzz of excitement he always felt and the blood pump through to his penis. His penis even seemed to twitch in unison with the crawl of the beast; the beautiful beastie with its mesh of the organic with the robotic. O how proud was The Catcher. How proud he was.

The information was passed. The beastie understood; this difficult little creature had been mastered by The Catcher. And he remembered that this had been a wild crawlie - a true *rapithra thufri*. There was spirit in its brown organic body. There was a deep connection through to the original nature of Upper and subearth as well as the polluted lands that lay beyond; or the islands of disease where Uppers were excluded. Yes, The Catcher smiled with grim delight. For the creature had proved to be a match. And The Catcher liked to be tested - so long as he won.

'I shall go soon,' he said, 'do as I have ordered.' To the warder he said, 'Find me a white-body fight for the end of the second quarter.'

The warder nodded.

The Catcher wanted to enjoy himself before his creature struck; give him time to accrue more credit in accordance with the Laws. Of course white-bodying was illegal. Except for The Catcher nothing was illegal. He laughed. Thought about the girl in the long-hut. Thought about the woman's eyes and the Eloluc woman who would have fresh vision. Grasped the body of the beastie and thought long and hard upon his mastery of it. And laughed out loud.

Chapter 15

Walking through Wayland I concentrated my thoughts on all that had gone wrong. Thoughts of the blackmailer turned my stomach. Thoughts of my wife simultaneously softened me and made me feel braver. People milled around, aimlessly it seemed. I felt in my pocket for dob - I hadn't much left but I needed to eat.

Disappearing into one of the subs' shops I bought more black bread and a couple of sorry looking apples. I was told I was lucky. The day was becoming brighter, a hint of warmth. Deep winter lay ahead. Exmass loomed. I had no idea if the subs underwent Exmass. What was there for them to spend and what could they buy? In Upper we had no idea why we celebrated Exmass - its historical roots had long since been severed. But it was a period of great excess (it was sometimes called *excess-mass*) and the chance to push one of the Life's Laws; we might overstep our boundary. But at a time of great spending and consuming what could the miserable of su do?

Coming back onto the main road, which began to narrow between squashed-together houses, I heard a sound I had thought alien to subearth - a kind of music. Approaching through the crowd I saw a group of subs chanting something and playing coarse-skinned drums. It wasn't a pleasant melodic music but there was a sense of defiance about the sound they created. I stopped to look, was careful to observe the attitudes of my "fellow" subs so not to look too interested and out of place. One of the crowd - who was dressed in heavy brown blankets and had knotted wild-looking long hair - came to me.

'Brother,' she said.

I looked around before answering, 'Greetings.'

'Are youse sure you will cross the Bridge brother?'

I smiled and then nodded, glanced about me. I noticed the brooch fastening the blanket upon the girl; a spider with its legs splayed.

'Be sure to be on the Bridge brother, it is written in the *"Thufris"*, *Leg One*: *a'ba dee m'none* - all who feels their ways in the dark shall cross the black river.'

I smiled again. The drums thudded in the background. A rhythm of sorts took mastery; tumtat/taratara/tumtat/bombbomb. The girl's eyes shone from out of her dirty hair that hung like jungle creepers (the sort found in Northern Upper). I noticed then a terrible scar running from her left ear to her chin.

'You want to cross the great Bridge brother?'

Playing safe I said, 'Yes.'

'Then follow. Swallow. Hollow. Follow brother,' she laughed. 'Make the *thufri* dance with us. Pull out the horizon-poison.'

I went to move away.

'Think of the animals in the western, desert; think of the eyes brother. Think about reaching the Great One across the Bridge. Oh, Bridge of sorrow and hope.'

'Yes,' I faltered.

'Think of those who call-fall to thems beds-deaths brother. Will you dance?'

I smiled yet again.

'Will you dance?' she spat.

I backed off. And she turned round before me and fixed a terrible set snarl upon her features, beginning to turn rapidly round.

'The *thufri*,' another sang up. 'The *thufri*,' others joined in and the whole of the procession began to turn. The blankets swirled about them like dirty ball gowns; a collection of horribly disfigured subs trailing behind. Ordinary subs remained impassive, began to disappear. So did I. But I looked back once or twice to convince myself I had actually witnessed that scene.

I walked on aimlessly, wishing time away, thinking only of meeting the man who had brought me so low. The streets even began to appear familiar - I knew roughly where the Mission was, and could always use landmarks like the chimney to help find it. Occasionally I nipped into doorways or behind walls to tap information into my digital and keep record of what had happened. The digital could still not pick up information from the Upper skies – perhaps that was lucky.

The last time I had urinated I had seen into a sub's house and caught a glimpse of "family" life. An old lady (though perhaps she was closer to my age than she looked?) was screaming incoherently at a boy child who had lacerations across his face. In the same room I saw a double bed with two people beneath its heavy covers. Were they the father and mother? Were they producing the next victim of the disease? Prurient as I had become I could not resist looking through all the windows on the first level. There was a girl who could only crawl across the floor of a room and in another - much cleaner room - a boy was being pampered by two other girls. The boy was sitting upright and looked almost angelic; the girls walked stiff-limbed and one had fingers missing from both her hands. The girls attentively groomed the lucky sub - a perfect little boy and yet not like a little boy at all (and as yet safe from the long-huts).

Later, as I turned down a narrow alleyway out of curiosity and to tap in more information, I was called into a doorway by a sleazy looking sub. I should have ignored his entreaties but a kind of boredom and inquisitiveness led me to him.

'Youse look al-reet,' he grinned. His teeth were blackened stumps and his breath reeked even from quite far away.

'Greetings.'

'Youse got dob? Don't ee worry, straight I am. Youse got dob or no?'

'Aye.'

'Come. No fear now. Do business. Got some weedle. Good stuff - eight thou, try it first friend.'

I followed him into the gloomy building, feeling my gun wedged into my trousers' back pocket. My eyes kept alert but found the darkness blinding.

'You got dob?' he asked again, smiling.

'Aye,' I repeated.

The sub looked about, 'Ere, take.' He handed me a pipe. At first I hesitated to hold the thing. I began to see in the gloom and noticed the spittle-flecked lips of the dealer. I also saw that time had worn away the fingers of his hand like that of a leper's. But he handed me the pipe as if the numbness did not exist. I imagined tasting the disease on the pipe's stem.

'Smoke ee,' the man said.

I smoked. The rush hit me straight away, I had thought the effect would have been similar to the rough sub grog (Zee had given me strong measures in the Mission) but it was something more and completely different. He laughed as he watched the effect just a quick suck had had.

'You aina tried weedle?' he laughed.

'No.'

'You like?'

I moved my head and it felt as if it could turn a full circle; I could feel the connection of my skull to my neck; feel messages sent down the spinal column. And I also felt thoroughly invigorated; felt the whole of my foot as if the numbness did not exist. But I also felt a residue darkness, or rather a darkness welling up in the back of my brain as if things could turn nasty.

I shook my head.

'Youse donna like?' he asked with incredulity.

I shook my head.

'Shell you, you slurry-wipe,' he coughed out, taking the pipe. His nature darkening also.

Removing the pistol quickly I rammed it towards his body, 'Don't shell-holy fuck with me, you understand?'

Taking a step back he turned his head and I thought I heard him shout something. Out of the blackness I heard rustling sounds. I fired off the gun and its flare of light and sound of bullet made everything surreal. I realised I was able to track the trajectory of the bullet as it entered the void; and that I was able to see in the ignited dark all the faces from out of that dark. But the short gasp from the pipe was wearing off quickly and I became aware of the ache at the back of my skull where I had been slugged previously. Lashing out with my fist I smacked it into the face of the dealer. A cry came from the subs in the darkness. I had hit one of them who obviously still felt blood pumping through his veins.

In the alleyway I decided to head down rather than back and up in the direction I had entered. The noises of su, I hoped, would have masked the terrible echo of the bullet. I had no idea how much my distorted brain had exaggerated the sound. Running down the narrow path I witnessed subs slumped against the dripping sides of its walls. I had to jump over some of their bodies. Some of these subs still held pipes.

The farther I ran the more the numbness returned to my toe and I became horribly aware - as if for the first time - that the numbness had spread. With this knowledge I limped more than usual. Back from the black-bricked buildings I could hear raised voices. But a few discreet turnings took me into another world - or so it seemed.

The turnings I had taken confused me. But I had wandered into a part of Wayland that was rather different from the rest. There seemed to be plenty of industrious activity - subs loading and unloading wood; carpenters at work. There were row upon row of archways each holding an artisan of some description - candle making; leather tanning; blacksmithing. Even the subs that had to drag their bodies about did so with a grim determination I had not previously seen.

As I limped from archway to archway I began to split my inner vision between what I could now see and images from Upper. How in su there were hardly any advertising boards or flashing neon; how the people had "regressed" to a pre-technological era. But I knew that the government of subearth had been given technology. How poor the people were; how many more children there were in su; how much sadness and craziness and yet a kind of weird happiness I saw in some of the subs' eyes.

There was a shop at the corner of the square of archways and tables set within. It seemed curious this - almost luxurious. I went in apprehensively. But a sub welcomed me with a smile.

'Sit ee,' she said.

'Thank ee.' I watched her. From behind a counter I could see her take a jug of water and place it into a bowl. Then she took a small bar of soap and a pumice stone and began to scrub her hands and arms. From the difficulty she had I could see that her hands were numb and the pumice stone was dropped into the bowl many times. After this she took a towel and dried herself. As she did not look at me I watched the meticulous way she rolled her sleeves down using the backs of her hands. And the way she fastened the cuffs (though I couldn't tell the device used for this at that stage).

She came over to me balancing another bowl upon her wrists and lower arms. 'Greetings,' she said.

'Greetings.'

'You'll want to wash-up.' She placed the bowl on the table. With ease she also placed down the towel the bowl had rested on.

'Aye.'

Her eyes twinkled keenly. 'You'unt not from this part?'

'No.'

Again she eyed me - intelligently I thought.

'You'unt from where?'

'From near the border,' I said.

'You have'unt a strange enough accent.'

I thought the way she spoke strange too - different from any other sub I had heard. Perhaps closer to Zee's accent in su.

'Yes,' I said.

'No matter,' she replied. 'You'unt want to drink grog or spice?'

I had no idea what spice was. 'Spice,' I said.

'And eat?'

'Whatever you have,' I replied.

She looked at me closely; looked my body up and down. 'Youse (I heard a change in her way of speaking) not a snatcher or govern-man?'

'No.'

She looked at me closely again.

'I am not,' I stated boldly.

She smiled.

'Eat something fresh,' she smiled, 'if you'unt've the credit. Somethin' fresh and hot.'

'Aye, please,' I said smiling. And for the first time felt myself relax slightly.

I washed my hands in the bowl with the soap and pumice stone as the sub had done. It felt good to be clean. I realised then that I probably smelt. I had not washed since arriving in subearth and the clothes I wore (including the jacket Zee had given me) had soaked up plenty of body fluids. These clothes had kept me anonymous in the rest of Wayland but now I felt self-conscious.

The waitress (owner?) came back with a glazed mug of spice. 'Heres you go,' she smiled. There was only one gap between her otherwise perfect set of teeth. I sipped at the drink, which was tepid. It lived up to its name being hot flavoured and spicy, but different in strength to the drink Zee had given me. It infused my body and mind with a gentle feeling of euphoria – chasing out any remnants of the weedle.

After the spice I was brought the steaming food, served in a dish and with a large metal spoon to ladle the thin stew up to my greedy mouth. I didn't know the origin of the meat - it was rare for us to eat meat like that in Upper. It was as I ate that I realised how necessary to the spirit was such wholesome food. But I cared not to think about the animal, where it was from or how it had been slaughtered.

As I ate I looked out onto the square at the subs toing and froing about their business. Occasionally subs without legs would roll into the square on wheeled platforms or be dragged on sledges ploughing into the earth or dust. These would be chased away by the more industrious subs - it seemed a hierarchy operated, at least in this part of Wayland. In the square there were no sex-subs either. Women and girls appeared to ply their trade through other parts of the sprawling town.

The waitress/owner came to me.

'You'unt want tea?'

'Tea?' I was astonished that she could serve such a drink.

'Aye, please,' I said. And for the first time too I wondered where our tea came from that we drank in Upper. I was ignorant – deliberately ignorant – of so much. I thought not just about tea but many things that we so readily consumed in Upper.

She smiled. Came back a few moments later and put a boiling pot of tea before me. I noticed her hands, though crippled by the disease were very clean. And the digits that remained had well manicured nails.

'Drink,' she said.

The woman received my credit and the extra for service with her beaming smile. I asked to visit the slurry. It was the cleanest I had seen in subearth and I only wished the black bread and the recent stew could have done their business; it would have been a pleasure to have squatted over that slurry-hole.

The rest of my time I tried to keep to myself and not to attract attention. I hid in derelict buildings or amongst the degenerate weedle users or the heavy grog merchants. I put up with the rats and the centipedes and all the filth that covered most of Wayland. I kept an ear open for the sounds of people and an eye on the light in the sky. I pissed against moss-covered walls and finally had a terrible slurry-shat in a pen occupied by a filthy looking pig.

One conversation I overheard talked about the markets to be found at the borders in the south of the country and the goods that could be illegally imported from Upper. Also talk of the scams used by the so-called government of su to keep for itself most of the handouts from the middle government of Upper. There was also chat about white-bodying; where it was going to take place next or what had happened during the last fights. It was overhearing one of these conversations that led me to go to fights arranged in a part of Wayland close by. Simple curiosity?

The watchers were as I expected them; furtive, shifty-eyed, dirty looking. I paid with metal dob and got to sit in the make-shift arena close to one of the trainers. I was asked if I wanted to see at the back, but I declined. It was bad enough that I was there, but the clouds were coming in fast and I sensed rain and cold winds.

For the sake of appearances I bet on two serpents and a turtle; I lost overall. The sight of the clumsy bodies with their occasional moments of lightning flash moves, the subdued horror of their felt pain and the dusty blood and bits of flesh scattering the saw-dusted floor made me fell ill. Just as I was about to go I noticed on the far side of the arena a man obviously from Upper. I noticed a flashing in his eyes, which travelled the two lengths from him to me. Something about this man's appearance unnerved me horribly. His brow was broad and his figure wiry. His posture seemed superior. I left quickly as a serpent's head flew through the darkened air.

Outside, the evening was beginning to come on. It was well on its way to the fourth quarter. I was ready to make my way back to the Bell Sisters and the showdown I was sure would ensue. But each step I made made me feel uneasy, as if someone was tracking me. Was it someone? I kept looking over my shoulder. But only rats scuttled from my trail. Yet a tingle ran up and down my spine. I experienced some of the hellish exaggerated reality of the weedle (it flashed-back) and drowsiness from the grog drunk at the white-bodying. I kept seeing the chalky bodies and the empty-eyed faces of the fighters. The noise of the crowd filled my ears and mind. Again I had the instinct to turn. Again it was as if shadows of men or creatures just disappeared from my sight. Oh how I longed for peace. How I longed for the soft touch of my wife.

Closer to the Mission I suddenly ran down a dusty road. The limp almost disappeared as subs watched me curiously; adults didn't run in that place. Fires burnt all around me. I hid down a few steps and ducked under some corrugated sheeting. I don't know why I did what I did; only that a tremendous and irrational fear had overcome me. *But I was in hell after all.*

Chapter 16

'He's been here,' Zee blurted.

'But he *is* coming back?'

'Yes.'

'Good.'

'I'm not sure anymore,' she said.

'It's too late.'

'He's told me things,' she said.

'What things?'

'He's got me some shots; he's been to the same doctor you went to. He told me the doctor told him everything about you. He told me that he killed the doctor. Needed to for the shots - oh holy-fuck shell.'

'Where are the shots?'

'I've taken them. I'm going to go back with him. He said he's just gone to sort some things out.'

'You don't need shots – you're a helper…'

'Not any more…'

'But you don't have the disease.'

'I'll be checked for shots – my blood – in Upper; if I get stopped – if I have to go through a screen and don't have helpers' papers. You know that. Dag knows what we'll do now. Maybe we'll get Adam…'

'The holy-shell but he's screwed things up hasn't he? He didn't need to kill the doctor. You could have gone back as a helper.'

'But they know all about us. They know about you and me. I'll have to pass myself off as an Upper. He knows that. He killed the doctor for me.'

'You're fooling yourself.'

'We'll see,' she said, her voice tense and shaky.

The thug who I had seen before came through to where Zee and I were.

'What?' she said sternly.

'He's a comin'.'

'Shell,' she spat, 'holy-shell. Youse'll have to hide. Can't have any more blood. Dag. Try to understand I just want my baby to be safe, to have a chance in this life...In Upper or…'

'There's no time for talk,' I cut her short. Quickly I hid inside the lower half of a huge chest. Through the keyless hole I was able to scan much of the room. I waited for the bastard-arachnid to arrive.

When he came in the room I almost gasped. It was Johnny. My friend. My work-mate. Johnny. We had worked together on the Register for nearly two years. I had given the man tips about share-shuffling. I had arranged for this man to visit a top massage-club in Upper. I had even used my connections with the Commander. My wife had fed him at dinner-parties. He'd drunk our wine. He was my *blackmailer*. And I was about to burst out of my crouched position and tear into his dirty-arachnid flesh. When. When he slumped into the arms of Zee. So I kept quiet and listened – for a moment.

'What's wrong Johnny? Speak to me.'

'Can't...' he spluttered.

'What has happened?'

I kicked open the chest at this point waving aside Zee's protestations. Taking him by the hair I looked into his eyes but already the life he had, had left them. I was robbed of the chance of confronting him. I wanted to hurt him, to make him feel pain - mental and physical. But neither Zee nor I could keep him from crashing to the floor. His body started to twitch and grow rigid, as if *rigor mortis* was setting in at speed.

'What's happened?' she screamed.

The thug entered.

'Shell-off!' I shouted. He still came towards me. I took the gun from behind me and went to blast a bullet between his eyes. The gun clicked - the chamber was empty. But Zee must have thought quickly and tossed me her own fire. The thug was almost upon me as I pulled the fire's trigger. Blood filled the gaping hole as the bullet entered the thug's eyeball and socket. He tumbled forward close to Johnny. Zee was on her knees by her lover. Then I heard her scream.

A beastie crawled over one of Johnny's legs.

'Mother-of-scales,' I shouted.

Zee screamed again. I slapped her hard across the face. 'Come with me,' I said.

'No!'

'It's the work of a catcher,' I said. 'The shots can't be good. Johnny hasn't been taking any shots,' I quickly explained. 'He's holy-fucked everything, can't you see? If he had had shots the beastie wouldn't have killed him (though I was unsure of the power of its venom and imagined it could have). Dag knows what he's being doing with the dob he's squeezed out of me. He's been as reckless as me – can't you see? Leave him. Krenz has fooled him but paid with his life. You've been duped...Duped! We've got to act *now*. We must kill that thing.' I took the gun and let off the remaining rounds at point-blank. The organic nature of the beastie exploded but the rest of it - its robotic components - remained in tact. 'We have to go, come on' I shouted. At that moment some of the Sisters tore into the room. They wailed high pitch and began laying into my body with tight fists.

'We have to run for it,' I shouted at Zee, catching her hand and kicking and slapping my way through the Sisters. Zee dragged half-unwilling behind me but not wholly unwilling. In the darkened air of the late third quarter or early fourth we suddenly stood motionless. I said, 'He's out there, maybe - The Catcher himself. He'll kill us both...'

Zee shook her head, but I guess she understood enough. Everyone had heard of the catchers; of *The Catcher*. Of the demon angel. Of Lord Satan?

We ran till our lungs stung. All the while Zee resisted enough to make the escape harder than it should have been.

'Don't you see,' I said, 'that should have been me back then. Or it should have been both of us. The Catcher doesn't get these things wrong. You're implicated beyond reason – you've admitted it yourself. We have to get the holy-fuck out of this dag place before another of those bastard creatures comes hunting us down. It wasn't dead. It isn't dead. You understand? The Sisters will tell everything.'

Zee collapsed against the side of a building. 'I only want to be with my baby,' she said.

'And me.' My answer seemed ambiguous.

'I trusted that man. I trusted him to sort things out, get clearance. I know he loved me,' she cried.

'Well,' I began tentatively, 'either he did or...' I felt some pity for her and continued, 'Are you going to run the risk of exposing yourself with what he's given you? The doctor's giving bent stuff. Must have. Or the beastie is stronger than I thought. If you go to Upper and the shots are false they'll know – then dag knows what they'll do with you. You think the long-huts are bad? You'll see what's *bad*.' She calmed a little – or she petrified. I continued, 'I only know it was Johnny who blackmailed me. You haven't got a clue,' I spat, 'and now he's dead and I probably ought to be. And I haven't got shots in my body – neither bad nor good. Holy-fuck. Somewhere out there a catcher, dag help us, will be tidying that dirty arachnid up and sending it off after me. You can't escape, you know. You can not escape. And it'll target you then too. They're gone Zee - all your plans have gone. The only thing to do is *escape*. To the mystery lands; take me there.'

'I can't,' she said.

'Why not?'

'I don't know if they exist - truly. I'm not certain. I haven't *been*.'

'But you said.'

'I'm not sure...It's one thing to be told, another to see with your own eyes, eh? I'm not sure I believe anything right now.'

But I thought she knew all right. I thought she knew.

Some subs got too close to us. I screamed at them. A one-legged sub made for me. I kicked away his crutch and stamped on his head.

'Let's try to find them, okay?' I said firmly.

'I have a contact, maybe,' she said heaving in breaths. Tears had streaked down her face. Her life like my life had been turned upside down. 'But I'm not sure. That's why I wanted my son to have the life of an Upper – I could be sure of that,' she hissed. 'That's why I took the risks I did. Besides – he is half-Upper…' I had never heard speak in that way before and I was shocked.

As we made our way through Wayland, aware of the ground beneath us for fear of a lurking beastie - or surfaces everywhere which we, and they, might rest upon, Zee talked more about Johnny.

'It isn't exactly how you think – Johnny and me.'

'How do I think?' I said caustically.

'He wanted to get Adam back from the adopters; he knew he couldn't do it through Records. It had to be done with hard credit. I'm sure that's why he faked having shots, *if* he faked having them,' she added. 'He told me he was doing everything he could to get money to get the baby back and me a true Upper identity. That's why he was screwing the shell out of you. You see, all three of us could have led the good Upper life. If he went without shots it was for me and our baby. That's love,' she spat.

'That makes me feel a whole lot better,' I sneered.

'This way,' she huffed and took me by the arm.

'He was out for himself, admit it...Admit you got it all dag wrong.'

'No! Why did he kill the doctor? Something must have gone wrong.'

'He killed the doctor to shut him up...simple as that.'

'You don't know that...he loved me...loves Adam. You don't know anything for sure. He loves me – loved me,' she added wistfully as if suddenly aware he was truly dead.

'Love?'

'Yes love,' she said.

'That's one thing I haven't seen much of in this dag-forsaken hole...'

'Adam's alone,' she cried out. 'My baby is alone.'

She took me through the usual maze of Wayland houses and streets. I tried to think about what a catcher would do. How long would it take to reprogram a beastie; or program another crawlie? Or did they carry more than one of the creepy things? I hated the idea of *raths*. The reality of them was harder to imagine - but there were other crawling things in the worlds of Upper and subearth. It didn't take much to combine the reality of the grubbing insects of Upper with the folklore passed from generation to generation. And, if you wanted, it was possible to see spiders in all their forms - including alive. (An example of a *rapithra thufri* – a dag *rath* was kept in Pointville.)

Stories had been written and flics with simulants made, there was even a Lifescene (copyright Leon and Co.) available. You could put yourself back in time and scare the living daylights out of yourself by interacting with various creepies. There were children's songs too:

Creepy, creepy spider, crawling up the wall

Creepy, creepy spider dangling overall

Along comes a baby with its mouth open wide

Creepy, creepy spider drops itself inside.

Or:

Spider in the bathroom, spider in the bed

Spider in the toilet, waiting to be fed

Spider crouching in its web or dangling out its feet

Spider waits to bite you as you sit upon the seat.

Or:

We are singing, we are singing, we can run and play

We are running, we are running, we can last all day

When a spider bites a body, its eyes can only stare

When a body has the numbness, we must all beware

Feel this, feel that (the children then kick and punch!)

Catch a spider with a rat (and one of the children becomes a spider to be chased by all the others).

Everyone but the catchers was terrified of the beasts. There were still organised spider hunts and on the last Vendredi of Feb'n'ary the children of Upper (and probably subearth) dress up as spiders or rats and chase around the houses. A bonfire is built and lit and a huge mock spider burnt upon it. Finally food in the shape of rats and spiders are cooked and eaten. (Many years ago fireworks were let off.)

Thoughts crossed my mind as we quickened or slowed our pace. I trusted Zee again. I had to. What else could I do? But there was the constant, nagging feeling that she might betray me. We both became terrified of the future. Of what it might throw from its dark shadows. Of the eight-legged monster that might have been prowling us at that very moment. Of a catcher or *The Catcher* letting the beast go close to where we were. Of the creature's tenacious pursuit - its legendary pursuit of its victims. And I was sure it would kill me. I was a transgressor. I was condemned.

We found our way to Zee's house where she explained the danger her mother might be in because of their relationship. The mother appeared quite calm, but gave me disdainful glances. How could things have ended the way they had? Tears of frustration wetted my eyes. How could things not turn out well? In Upper we believed in things turning out well. In Upper we believed in the fairy-tale. Of the crushing of the dirty spiders – the end of all *raths*.

I just couldn't believe that the way things were developing were so at odds with the plans I had had. In my mind I had truly thought I would get some shots and be together, be reunited, with my wife in Upper. That everything would have been sorted out. That I might have learnt from my reckless past. Even that Zee and her child would have been reunited. Perhaps I would have killed Johnny and screwed the doctor for everything he had. But that wasn't life. Life had a way of screwing up endings so they spat back in your face. Life could take a part of you and squash it into a deadly void. Or create some horrific reality that seemed like infinite torment. I only wanted to open my eyes and see that nothing had happened - that I was lying in my bed with my wife by my side and a healthy baby in its cot.

We stayed a short a time as possible. We needed to move – *fast*.

Outside again we rested under yet another crumbling walled shelter. The subs seemed crazier than ever. The moon was almost full. Dimanche was on its way. In the eerie light we imagined a spider sticking its dirty little legs across the detritus of the floor. Feeling us in its un-human way; The Catcher calling out to it like a man possessed - like a fucking holy-roll-shell demon. But we heard only the slither of rats as they trailed their naked tails through the slurry-crap that littered the inside of the place.

Outside you could hear the subs going crazy. Words mixed up; words put in places no words belonged. I wanted them to chew on their own words and swell their tongues so they clogged their throats. I wanted vomit to suffocate them. I had little sympathy for anyone but myself – and my pregnant wife – and maybe Zee.

We sweated and panted out tainted breath.

'We'll have to go,' I said.

'I want to drink,' she said.

'Later. You should have drunk at your house.'

'The shell later,' she spat. 'I'm holy-fuck dying.'

'How far?' I said.

'Out of Wayland and across country,' she said.

'How long?'

'Not so long...'

'Good.'

She looked at me with venom in her eyes, as if it were all somehow my fault.

'Come on,' I said, 'you know that bastard will be sniffing us out. You know. A catcher's never going to stop. You know. A beastie never gives up. That's the fuck-slurry way...'

'That's the way of you all,' she said.

'What do you mean?'

'You're all the same...'

'Shut the shell up.'

Then we carried on. I pushed subs out of my way; kicked over a brazier and watched it roll down a road sending out its sparks of fire; watched the subs either yell out in pain or stare at their melting flesh without feeling - their eyes befuddled. I hated the damn place. I hated the damn disease. I hated the world I came from. But I still looked at the body of Zee as she led me on.

When we reached the last straggling huts of Wayland (there were no long-huts there) I was mesmerised by the moon and the stars. Though the countryside was scrub beyond, there was a kind of pale beauty. This beauty gave me some hope; some reason to think life was worth struggling for again. Zee turned to me and in the moonlight I could see her eyes blaze up in a kind of animal fire. It was a strange experience and the sense of it quickly dissolved. I turned back to Wayland and witnessed the fires belching out their smoke and the wails of the lunatic subs brought to a desperate madness by an incurable disease.

* * *

The Catcher reached the Mission and saw the barely flinching body of his beloved. The Sisters cowered from him; curtsied in his presence. The young girl took him grog. The Catcher examined the body of Johnny. Yes he was a government worker. Yes he worked for Records. Yes he worked on the Register. And was not he the one who had killed the yellow-toothed Doctor?

But he was not Adam X.

The *rath* had had its organic body mashed into the fibre of Johnny's clothes. The Catcher swept up what was left and tucked it into his pocket. There was not much time; but time had to be made. Time to heal the creature or time to sweat on the palm of his hand whisperings to his newest beastie – a beastie eager to prove itself. The

Catcher did not like to lose. An image stole across his mind. A face in the gloom of a white-bodying arena.

The Bell Sisters busied themselves about his taut features – his gangling frame; saw to his every whim. Eloluc sponsored spies came to give him messages, spat at the Sisters as they entered the female haven. Bowed to the Master catcher. The two rebels were making their way out. The Catcher would have to work fast. The rebels must be Pandlams. Must be working to overthrow the government of su. The Catcher listened only vaguely as he whispered to the new beastie on his palm. Had he failed? *Had he failed?*

The Catcher recalled the sight of a white-bodying fight. The slicing off of a chalk-body's hand. A trickle of blood maybe. And a look from the serpent's eye that had...concerned him. He had waited till the very end inside the door marked "To the White Rooms". Had seen the solemn looking serpent's eyes as he entered. And stepping through, it was he (the Master catcher) who had applied the delicate push to send the *seemingly* paralysed body – the victorious fighter - into acidic oblivion. Yet. Hadn't the dirty sub risen from the acid one last time and held the stub of his arm aloft? And hadn't there been a look upon the featureless face - in the doomed eyes? The Catcher (don't even whisper this) shuddered slightly.

As the Sisters tended to the fire and to his needs, The Catcher seemed to gaze into the future. Something greater was at stake. Something greater than the meaningless life of a transgressor.

Chapter 17

We made it across the open country with the feeling that nothing could have kept up with us. But I knew too that a catcher could use any kind of transport he wanted to cut us off. But Zee had mellowed, and I saw something of her old self, or what I took to be her better nature.

'I did love him,' she said to me, 'no matter what you think. He gave me the chance to get out of this place. I couldn't have got a helper's place without him you know. I realise how much you must hate him but...'

'But what?'

'Well, to begin with, he only said good things about you...'

'We were kind of friends,' I laughed sourly.

'Things got out of hand. We didn't expect me to get pregnant...'

'No,' I smiled not unkindly.

She looked at me with more sympathy then, I felt. She said, 'It must be hard to be away from your wife.'

'It is.'

She looked at me for a very long time then said, 'In some kind of way this is all my fault isn't it?'

'No,' I said involuntarily.

'Yes,' she said quietly.

Dawn began to rise. We were weak and longed for drink or food. Occasionally I would turn my back on Zee and log information into my digital. Why I would want to show my trail I didn't know - it gave me a false sense of being in control. Light spread across the horizon; the beginning of the second quarter of my last day as a free-man. It was the way I viewed it. I was no longer a part of Upper but su had not entirely swallowed me up either. Not completely. And I wanted to ask Zee about how she and Johnny had got together – but I couldn't think about him without feeling either hate for what he had done to me and my life or sadness that he had died. These were contradictory and unsettling feelings that I needed to bottled up.

Zee said, 'You know I *wanted* to lie with you...'

I laughed cynically. You *did*.'

She looked bewildered for a moment, 'No,' she said, 'I mean in bed, next to you, I wanted to make *love* with you...' She said these words both boldly and yet shyly.

I looked at her deeply. The light was penetrating the darkness of the past day. The light was glorious and luminescent. Powerful and delicate. Trees silhouetted against the ripening colours looked bold and permanent. There was a great rolling hope crashing against the horizon - a wave of fresh colour thickening its hues and intensity. I looked deep into Zee's eyes and sensed a great unhappiness and perhaps a longing to be good and true. Her honesty then surprised and shocked me. And also it didn't shock me at all.

'You have the disease because of me,' she said.

'Because of a crawlie.'

'Because of me…'

I had the disease. I truly had the disease. But it wasn't possible. No. Dag. It couldn't be. I was still partly in denial. That was funny. That was sick. That was hope springing eternal…

She took me to a house that stood out on a hill some four hundred lengths (forty leagues) from the outskirts of Wayland. The day was warming up as we entered through a back door. Inside I met men and women with smiling faces and demeanours different from any other sub I had ever met. More so than those I had seen working while I ate and drank at the house/café on the square.

Grog was handed out.

'Greetings.'

'Greetings,' I answered. I saw Zee fall into the arms of one of the men and I thought bad thoughts about her again. I also realised that the "mystery lands" couldn't be quite so mysterious.

'Take this,' a girl said, offering me a mug of grog.

'Eat this,' said another.

'You are known,' said a young man with a beaming smile. I smiled too. But I also saw that these subs suffered from the disease. And I saw that they were at pains to hide another sub in a back room. But he fought his way out crying, 'It's him; it be he; the angel; he's comin' he's a comin' to set us free...'

The others tried to restrain the fellow and to mask their embarrassment they smiled and joked much. But the man - not an old man - kept speaking loudly, 'It is he, canst youse all see? He beent here to set us upon the Bridge. To set us on the road home. Don't yese know yer history? Yers traditions? Yers culture of old? Has ye lost it all? It is the angel - the dark, magnificent angel...'

Before long I was being told of these people's struggle for independence from their own government and from the shackles of Upper. But they took me and all my inquisitive thoughts well. We talked and grog was passed amongst us. Young girls brought me food to eat. I was told of their exploits and their fierce battles. Men and women fought together - though the men told longer tales. And though some occasionally mixed up their words or forgot sentences half way through the disease had not caught them as bad at it might – yet. Perhaps those who could no longer think or talk rationally were…and I wondered exactly what their fate might be. Would these rebels with the disease show more compassion? I would find out.

Before long I was learning about their past and how the struggle to free Pandlam (as they called subearth) had been waged for many, many years. I learnt of their battles with the Upper Legionnaires. I learnt of their belief in a separate land for Pandlam away from its dependency on Upper. But they also wished to be treated as equals and to be allowed to manufacture their own shots and thus to begin the eradication of the disease. They were brave men and women whose exploits had been censored by both Upper and su governments and press. Was it simply my ignorance or position that meant I had never heard of Pandlam? Or had I seen or heard that name before?

While I listened to the impassioned voices and their disgust for the body-part trade and white-bodying, and the long-huts (they didn't seem to believe the bodies were "angles") I was hardly aware of the sun's rise in the heavens. Hardly aware of emotions stirring within me. And totally unaware of the whereabouts of Zee. True to her word she had led me to safety, but true to herself she had cast me aside for the attention of the young warriors.

The youngest of the men were keen to ask me all about the Upper world and I could see that they were part disgusted and part intrigued by my descriptions. Though they hated the injustice of the privilege we experienced I could also see that they ached to live my type of life (before my fall - and not working for the corrupt Eloluc). I was surprised how much prejudice they had and how much false information. Even as we talked they integrated their newly found knowledge of Upper in a creative but quite negative fashion. Yet they had a refreshing and infectious openness I presumed lacking in the lifeless subs of Wayland. And they seemed to me to be prepared to struggle against the insidious spread of the numbness and the horror of the shrinking mind.

The Pandlams (as I called them) showed me some of their kind who had been stricken by the disease and who were in its latter stages. Rather than discard these people or send those with young or intact bodies to the long-huts, they tried to stimulate their minds with games and practices in art and music. These Pandlams were only the second set of subs I had seen who delighted in sound (and I wasn't sure how much the *Thufris* – the crazy dancing sect - delighted themselves).

But the sight of those at the end of the disease was always so distressing; no control over their frozen bodies; excreta clogging their clothes and the smell of urine; the rambling talk or the lack of any talk - the lack of any seeming consciousness; an eternal trapped present. Minds without memories. Waiting to die. Waiting for oblivion. And unlike the subs in the long-huts all these Pandlams seemed to have bodies mutilated by the disease.

I saw a young man with eyes still bright but whose mouth hung limply and whose lips were torn and ineffectively sewn back into place. I saw the ravages of past diseases taking vengeance upon an almost dead immune system. Rashes and boils scarring most of the young and old skin. But Pandlam's carers had not given up on him or any of the others. Even in the midst of fighting a bitter guerilla war – they had energy for concrete - true - compassion.

'The beast is at the gate, the beast is at the gate,' one poor old woman moaned, rocking at the same time.

But the Pandlams seemed always gentle with these diseased people - did not make it obvious that they were scared of the disease. Those who had been spared its contagion got their hands as dirty as any other. No-one had asked if I had the disease, I did not know if Zee had told them, I supposed it was obvious; why else would an Upper be down so far? I wasn't loitering at the border doing dirty business – was I?

I wondered if a slow mental and bodily death was the way a brave man, one of their fighters, might die. Could so much courage, then so much effort and so much resistance end in it all being wiped away? Of course death scared me, but to lose memory before death...to lose oneself before death. The men and women who struggled and fought could all die as rambling, insane old folk (old if they were lucky!); unable to move a limb of their body - slurry-arsed. Again I looked at the young man with the stricken face. I thought about my child growing in Jo's womb. Everything brought my mind back to that new being. I wanted freedom for him. Freedom from oppressive rules; freedom from disease. I laughed. Until recently I had been a "good" man - a man of the government. Now I was ready to become a rebel.

The effect of the food and drink and all the sights I had seen lulled me to sleep. And I was not woken. Though the sun had risen and a fresh wind blew over the barren lands and grassy hills of that part of su, I slept soundly. When I awoke, I realised Zee had gone.

Of course I didn't want to believe so. I didn't want to believe that she could have done such a thing. But she had slipped from the rebel base and had been seen heading back to Wayland. I just couldn't believe things could be so...I thought she might have changed. I really and truly thought she might have changed. But she was gone. *Gone.* And, I supposed, would not come back.

After more drink and food I was taken by a tall, good-looking Pandlam to an office away from the main clutch of buildings. He said that he could get me out of Pandlam (he actually called it su!) if I wished. I knew I would have to get to the mystery lands before I could make contact with my wife again. There had to be somewhere safe. Somewhere away from the insanity of our "perfect" life. Somewhere I could take her and my child. I agreed. It was decided the two of us would go the next day. By Lundi everyone in Upper would know of my fate.

I spent the rest of my time getting to know people and asking about their life away from the main towns of subearth. And I talked to an old man who had the disease but whose mind had remained clear.

'How long have you lived here?' I asked him.

'Many, many years...'

'What changes have you seen?'

He laughed. 'Enormous. You'unt...youse,' he changed, 'would hardly recognise this land from my youth. The disease has weakened this generation's revolver, ugh, sorry,' he thought for awhile, 'resolve, yes, to fight. Understand ee? It is only these'm who have the courage. Reminds I of my time as a young'un; thought we got make a difference...' he smiled inwardly. 'Now this holy-disease has frozen me up. Youse see? And you be unt an Upper. Not the first I seen...maybe the last,' he joked.

I shook my head.

'These'm good men,' he whispered, 'good men. Good men in Upper too, eh?'

I nodded and thought. Was I a good man? Would he have talked to me knowing my history?

Before sleeping that night I patted my torso and felt for my digital. Gone. I quickly stripped off my top clothes - but it was not there. I panicked, flushed - there was a brief moment when I thought it all a nightmare, but it was true, it had gone. Had someone stolen it?

Had I mislaid it somewhere? No I had not taken it off. I would never have done that. Even when I had taken a shower I had kept it taped to me. It was the way. When had I taken that shower? I felt disorientated suddenly, wondered if someone had slipped me some weedle - it was a dishonourable thought.

I looked around the room where I was to sleep that night. Nothing. The digital kept me linked; and it would show me the way back - tell me everything. I felt lost without it. I felt truly vulnerable. I felt like a holy-shell sub. In shell subearth. Dag. Holy-fuck su. I kicked something. Looked again. But it was gone. I didn't know what to do, whether to accuse one of the Pandlams of theft. I was a guest, looked after. And these men and women were warriors. Sitting down on the bed I put my head in my hands and cried. I didn't feel much like a man. Everything had got too much. I wanted out.

* * *

The Catcher stepped over the seat of the hover-cycle and sheathed the rifle into its holster. It was an old-fashioned weapon but it gave him a kick to have it with him. He drove with his left hand, stopping occasionally to smell the air and to take the beastie from his pocket. As he rode his right hand would play with the creature. Talk to it through DNA. Would sing to it through the sweat of his skin. Such sweetly sung whispers.

Stopping the bike The Catcher dismounted and placed the beastie on the ground. He was receiving signals from Upper and from spies working within su. He wondered if he had made the correct decision in patching up the *rapithra thufri* that had killed the transgressor. But he believed in his beasts. Believed in the power of the ancient whisperings.

And so it was that he turned away from the creature as it scurried beneath the dirty su sun and headed back to the shambles that was Wayland. Only the orders of the Eloluc would see him abandon his beastie. But it brought a tear to his eye to think of the beautiful creature crawling across the earth and grass of that despicable place.

The bike glided over the barren earth and the patches of grass, which appeared like green and ghostly lakes. The Eloluc transmitted to him but the signal was weak and had to be picked up by his bike. He had so wanted to be there when the beastie bit into the transgressor's flesh. Sent its beauty rushing through the weakened blood of the outlaw. O how he wished to see that last moment of sanity before the terrible rush of realisation that madness was coming. A split moment of understanding - that complete irrationality that would swamp his mind. And a split moment later the frozen death, like the surface of a lake turned to ice.

The Catcher felt angry and cheated. Had thoughts of slicing through legions of chalky bodies. But it could be that he would - and he remembered an old Upper rhyme from his youth – "kill two spiders in a pot". Yet these people had none of the beauty and power of a spider, of a beastie, of a *rath*.

The sun was high. He roared the bike on, gritting his teeth, throwing back his head in glee almost, as if he were once again a young man.

Chapter 18

We set-off early on the Lundi. It was still dark. Reluctantly I left the comfortable bed - it was the first undisturbed night's sleep I had had since Upper (and those had been disturbed for some time). We went on foot for about a day's quarter. The countryside got steadily hillier and the going was tougher. The sun crept from behind banks of cloud every so often and I could see from the ground that there had been rain showers.

As the sun reached its zenith we passed between two huge slabs of rock. Beyond this pass the land opened up to a wide plain. A river glimmered in the distance and beyond that lay a range of mountains. I had had no idea such land existed.

'Beyond that mountain range,' said Oomac (my rebel guide), is the land you call the mystery lands. We call it Pangott. Some of our people have gone there. You will find people eventually.'

I looked at him and smiled.

The descent to the river took a half-quarter. At the banks of the wide flowing waters Oomac said to me:

'We must part here. Now you must walk to the foot of the mountains. Word has gone ahead; there will be another guide waiting for you. He will find you, have no fear. Before we depart though,' he dipped a hand into the sack he was carrying, 'take this. But don't open it until I am out of sight. Also, you might need this,' he took out a small revolver - a fire - to replace my pistol.

'Thank you,' is all I could say. But we embraced and I hoped he saw the gratitude and love that I carried in my eyes.

Great storm clouds seemed to gather over the distant mountains. I stopped and took a bite of black bread. I had cheese too (made from milk taken from the Pandlams' goats). Sitting down I opened the package Oomac had given me. There was a letter addressed to me; written in the script of subearth. I scrunched up my eyes to read:

'Dearest, noblest A - from your friend Zee,

Today I have gone from you and - forgive me - taken your digital. I am going to return to Upper, if I can, and give the digital to your wife. With everything you have recorded she will be able to find the Pandlams and eventually the mystery lands – yes they exist! I know what you must think of me, but don't judge too harshly. It's hard for one such as me to live in su. I have neither the mentality of the subs in Wayland nor the fighting spirit of the Pandlams. I am half Upper, perhaps. I am not fitted to be a helper; you can understand that. But though I have betrayed you with Johnny you must know how it feels to have something, someone, you love unconditionally, that you would do anything for. So it is for my baby. So it is for your unborn child. I would have done, and would still do anything for my baby. Perhaps you understand now - you certainly will understand. As for Johnny. He changed. He was a good man. Even though he worked on the Register. You can be a good man and work for Records you know. You know. So, I hope to make amends, to make some amends, for what you have been through. If one day you can live in simple peace with your wife and child in the mystery lands then perhaps it will all have been worthwhile. Perhaps one day I will join you. And Adam I want you to know that I do care for you. In a different world; at a different time perhaps things might have been different between us. Perhaps I am saying too much – our lives, our destinies, are very different. I thought I was to be an Upper woman married to an Upper man with our Upper baby. But now I must carry on my way – must find my child. Must hope I do not get betrayed or exposed as a common sub. Things will be difficult but I am determined to reach your wife. I still have friends and contacts in Upper. You would be surprised at what the Register does not know. I will put things right as well as I can. Your wife will know the truth. Then I must discover the whole truth of this strange life. Yes, I must find my Adam and be near him. And your wife and child will find you.

Your faithful one, I promise,

Z.

Spots of rain began to smudge Zee's writing – perfect, manual writing; I could have kicked myself. I opened my eyes as if to awake anew. Quickly I opened the package and there was another note there:

Adam - from Oomac:

Friend. Here is shot powder. You can eat it or smoke it. Best if it is in the blood but we have no razors ("syringes"). Good fuck my friend.

Yours in faith,

Oomac.

Long live Pandlam!

I had an idea. But first I needed to cross the river.

Tentatively I stepped into the river's water and began to wade across. At first the river seemed shallow enough but about a third of the way the bed of the river dropped steeply. The coldness rose up my body as if through osmosis. My trousers became sodden and the skin beneath achingly cold. Still I waded on and the depth of the water rose to waist height. By then I was finding it difficult to move through the current. The river seemed wider as I looked back to where I had come from, (which seemed relatively near) then across to the farthest bank. Because the water was so high it looked terrifyingly distant. And my limp became exaggerated in the water's flow.

The current was strong. The noise of the river frightened me. And I was surprised by my reaction - perhaps it was because I was so close to safety. Taking the plunge I swam out with one hand, the other holding my bag aloft. Desperately I fought against the river's flow and felt the iciness of the water spray against my face. The whole of my body and clothes became wet save for the arm held aloft. I could only manage a few strokes at a time in that fashion, having to stop to prepare myself once again. Above, clouds had rolled in heavily. I set forth again and again went to stop. This time my head went beneath the water, freezing my brain. I swallowed some water. The bag I clutched kept dry but I needed to push up with all my might and reserves of strength to swim on.

Kicking furiously with my legs (one foot almost dangling) I made enough headway across the current to avoid the river's greatest depth. When I tried my feet again (through absolute exhaustion) I found I was able to stand - though water lapped against my chin and froze my poor lips. With the effect of the cold water both feet felt absolutely numb.

Wading with wet clothes was more difficult than I had imagined but eventually I made it to the far bank. I threw down the bag I had carried so vainly and waited for the blood to circulate through my arm once again. This happened normally enough, thankfully. Lying down I stared up at the blackening heavens. Tiny drops of rain added to my soaking. I revolved the ankle of my infected foot and cursed the numbness that deadened my toes.

It must have been many moments that I lay down. The threatened downpour had still not arrived. Heaving myself up I began looking for a sharp piece of stone close to me. I found a perfect example. I washed the stone carefully in the waters. Rain still dripped down. Water still trickled from my clothes. I then took off my right shoe and sock; the smell was vile. Both were sodden of course. I gazed at the dirty wet bandage wound around both my toes and foot. Carefully I unwrapped this and revealed the pared flesh where I had cut previously. The whole of my foot seemed paralysed – not just the toes. I couldn't feel the blood circulate. Again I revolved my ankle as if to force the circulation. Placing myself on the bank of the river I let my foot dangle into the cold waters. The direct coldness only added to the sense of numbness. Was it true? Was the disease spreading? I had almost convinced myself it would spread no further.

Carefully I washed my naked foot and rubbed its sole over a smooth stone; it felt good. Then I lifted it out and placed it on an almost dry rock sticking up from the waters close to the side of the bank. I clutched the sharp piece of stone in my right hand. Gritting my teeth I gouged at the pared flesh of my big toe. The pain came through slowly - but there *was* pain. A shocking, intense pain that accumulated and grew as time passed. I tried to console myself that if there was pain there was also good blood. But the pain seemed lodged in my mind. If I were to pinpoint that hurt it would have been in the consciousness of my mind not the reality of my physical body. The features of Doctor Krenz flowed through my mind. Again I pulled the sharp rock into and through my skin. Following the trough of the original paring it bit into clean flesh. Blood began to rush out and the rock I had placed my foot on was soon crimson.

Next I took the powder, careful not to wet it (I had blown my hands near dry). And with an almost shaking hand rubbed the shot-powder in, pressing it into the newly opened wound. When I had pushed in all I could I rewound the dirty bandage. Prayed there would be no extra infection to the deadly one. The rest of the powder I dissolved into the remaining grog and drank in one draft.

Once my sock and shoe were back on I felt better. Though I was wet and uncomfortable I also felt secure. There was one unpleasant thought in my mind it was true, but I figured that that could wait until I had finally reached Pangott.

Walking (limping heavily to begin with) towards the mountains, the heavens opened and I became as soaked as when I had swam the river. In the distance though I could see snow glinting on the mountains and knew the sun would shortly come out.

I walked on. Trance like. Wet. Rubbing clothes. Aching foot. I walked, limped, on.

By the time I reached the foot of the mountains the sun had been out for a near half-quarter though already it was dipping towards the horizon. As I sat down to rest beneath a still leafy tree the guide Oomac had promised came calmly up.

'You must be hungry,' he said with a kind smile.

'Yes,' I smiled weakly.

'Greetings.'

'Greetings.'

It took a day and a night to cross the mountains. At times I had to lean heavily on my guide. Then, finally, we were in the mystery lands. There were people; there were rudimentary homes; there was freedom. Two days after arriving I tied a tourniquet to just below my knee and with a knife began to slice through my flesh. I asked the help of no-one. I could not burden those friendly people. A strong stick was placed into the heart of the fire I had made. I drank as much grog to make me braver than I was but not enough to lose concentration. Yes, I drank enough to hardly care for the pain but not so much that I didn't know exactly what I was doing.

The flesh was easily cut. Blood filled up the clean slice. Deep, almost black blood. When I reached the bone I felt close to passing out - but I knew my life depended on my courage and clarity of action. My will power to sever the leg. Removing the first blade I exchanged it for a saw-toothed blade (both borrowed for this gruesome act) and began to cut into the bone. All the while I bit down onto a piece of leather clenched between my teeth. There are few words that can describe such a monstrous act. Pain became transcendent. Transcendental. I hallucinated for a time - seeing animals move about the circle of light shed by the flames of the fire. I saw the face of Zee and the face of my wife. I saw an ape like creature with the face of Johnny. And I saw a spider greater in bulk than a man's head. And still I sawed. I sawed with a purpose that I did not know my reckless nature had. I sawed until the bone was snapped. Clean. The link of bone gone. Almost with a cool calculation I removed the saw toothed blade and returned the sharp bladed knife. The rest was easy. I cried. I laughed. I exalted. I climbed up into the stars. But I remained willful. And cut off my leg. Cut off my leg - completely. And I trusted my life was saved.

With the stick from the fire I rolled it over the exposed tissue and burnt it closed. I passed out on each occasion I tried to do this. It was then I felt gentle hands take hold of my head. My eyes swam and my lids closed heavily. I know now that the people of the village had boiled pitch and finished the job for me.

For three days I sweated and tossed and turned and shouted out meaningless, delirious sentences. I cursed and laughed. And I told rambling tales of my adventures. Children were shooed away as I rasped curses upon the day and night. But on the fourth day I was coherent enough to be given the first report.

The first report read:

There is news. There is news of Zee. She made it to Upper. Our people tell us that she made it to the wife of Adam. That she had crossed the border at one of the southern markets. Was taken over the border as a helper. Passed between households where the helpers controlled. Escaped when Patrons and Matrons suspected concealment. Finally reaching the house of Adam. But there were only helpers there and Zee understood that the wife of Adam had been taken into protection by her father, the dreaded Commander. But she carried on. Was undeterred by the danger. Though it took courage she made contact with the wife, proving her identity with the digital. Helpers from the Commander's household enabled both women to escape. The helpers were later killed. (But they had already begun the escape telegraph.)

The women were able to cross the border by means of a "disease pass". The wife of Adam had papers from the Commander from which our people forged the necessary documents. This is our full knowledge so far. We write in the tongue of the Upper; the dialect of the helper, for the man Adam.

Long live a Free Pandlam! Long live the Free Lands beyond the mountains!

I read the paper and then held it close to my chest. Sweat still beaded my brow. Fever had yet to release its tenacious hold. The next day I was handed a second report. The people of the village had been reluctant to give it me. But these people believed all information was valuable. Nothing known was to be kept unknown. The second report read:

The Catcher - last seen at the border crossing where the women left Upper.

Long live Pandlam!

There was something fateful unravelling in the land of subearth and I was powerless to act. But I determined to beat the fever and to restore my energy. I fixed my will again. I ate. I drank. And the craftsmen of the village sculpted me a false limb to be attached to my shortened leg.

With crutches fixed under my arm I made my first steps under the starlight. Jo and Zee were beyond the distant mountains. So was The Catcher and so were the beasties, I presumed. Campfires burnt - and the smell of cooked food perfumed the air. When Jo arrived (as I had dreamt many times in my imagination) I vowed we would set off further to the West and make a new life; a new hope; a new family; a new beginning.

A dog cried in the distance, it sounded lonely, forlorn. I too wanted to howl beneath the pock-faced moon.

Chapter 19

The spider made its way across the terrain of subearth; nothing prevented its eight-legged march. Its fused organic and robotic being was determined to find its prey. The beastie crawled through the outer edges of Wayland. No rat attacked it. No foot crushed it under a heavy sole. The beastie used cunning; used instinct and greater knowledge. Did its Master's bidding.

* * *

Each day was a torture without news of either Jo or Zee. But there was nothing anybody could do. And all I could do was walk with the artificial leg for as long as I could stand the pain - literally. For the stump of my leg, though cushioned by softened leather and wool taken from the sheep the people kept, was still soft and the pain agonising. But I bit my lip and continued to pace up and down. The children of the village played with me and through them I learnt much about the people's ways. I learnt too, that the villagers were not all migrants from su. That some were indigenous to the lands to the south-west. And I wondered why so few subs had trekked the way I had come. Why hadn't Zee come to these lands – was it Johnny who prevented her? Or was it that she had been beguiled by the possibility of life in Upper? Had she chosen a privileged life in Upper for baby Adam over freedom and integrity in Pangott?

From the "indigenous" children I heard stories of the hardships of their people and their distrust of the subs still living in subearth. They thought these subs preferred to live as slaves to Uppers rather than living free in a hostile land. I never heard their new home referred to as Pangott either. But these children and their families had migrated to Pangott – what had they left behind or fled from? Though I asked questions I received few answers. The children who came from the south-west territory and the children of Pandlam (su/subearth) seemed to mix well enough but there was clearly a difference in the way they and their people spoke and dressed and there were two differing cultures. The more I observed, the more I saw the distinctions between these cultures – but for the most part there was a unifying harmony and sense of purpose.

But I also learnt another fact. A fact that chilled me and made me see the people of the mystery lands in another light. For the older children told me that any sub who reached the mountains and had the disease would be instantly killed. And yet I was spared. I asked them how they knew if someone had the disease if they had yet to show the symptoms. The children (all of the children) said they had learnt to smell it. I was reminded of the dark skill of the helpers. It made me reflect differently on things. These were tough (but friendly) people who – perhaps simply to survive – had learnt to be ruthless.

Later I took courage to ask one of the village elders. He told me straight. Told me that there were those amongst his people who had the gift of smelling the deadly disease and that, indeed, if a diseased sub came to their lands they would be killed immediately. Only the rebels were allowed to the river bank. I thought of Oomac. Had Oomac the disease? I asked. The elder nodded his head. And I asked about myself - for surely they knew why I had cut off my leg.

The elder spoke:

'You are a lucky man, my beloved fellow. You'unt have been spared. The disease has died within thee.'

This news shocked me greatly. But I was near euphoric. The relief was blissful. After some time I spoke, asking, 'If the disease had lived within me elder, would you have killed me?'

'Of course my dear one,' he answered with smiling eyes.

That night I prayed that Jo and Zee were still clean. Had Zee not come to the mystery lands in case baby Adam had the disease (or might in five years)? Would they have killed a child who had grown amongst them if the disease eventually showed itself? Would they even take the risk of allowing children from su into Pangottt? Cynically I wondered if Pangott had its own White Rooms. But these were different people – though like Uppers they wanted above all to protect themselves.

That night I thought about the rebels and especially Oomac. How many of his men and women had the disease but with it still in its early stages? Was it the disease which, in a curious fashion, gave them courage? How many of his (clean) followers had deserted for the land beyond the mountains (or if not clean been slaughtered)? Or were there those who thought it best to stay and fight? How else could their vision of Pandlam be realised? In a sense it was a futile if noble struggle.

The third report I received read:

Yesterday, at the sun's zenith, the woman known as Zee was killed by The Catcher. It is bad news for all those who long for freedom - but it was her act of heroism that saved the wife of Adam. It is a great strike at the power of Upper that the daughter of a powerful legionnaire, a renowned commander, should escape to Pangott. The Catcher killed Zee not through the hated holy spider but through conventional fire. Men of Pandlam shield the wife of Adam and help her on her way.

Greatness shines on Pandlam - it shall rise from the diseased pit. Freedom!

Zee dead? Zee, the beautiful faced Zee, dead? I walked out beyond the boundary of the village to think. There was much - had been much - unsaid between us. I realised that for some deep reason, and not just her bravery and death, I loved her. And it seemed possible to love two women. That was the extent to which the petty government official had changed. I cried and howled into the night - and the dog in the distance howled back at me.

The night past fitfully. I knew that out there somewhere my wife, with our child in her belly, was trying to escape The Catcher. I couldn't help but think about the chances of the baby aborting through the stress and strain both it and Jo must be under. And I felt impotent to help. And yet that very same night of dreams and nightmares I made up mind to go back into subearth and try to find her. However crazy the idea might have been as soon as I made my resolve I felt stronger and braver. Perhaps it was a last act of genuine recklessness? A clean man goes into the land of the diseased. And in the country of the diseased the one-legged man is king!

There was no time for me to wait and I didn't want to hang around for a fourth report - I knew all too well what that might be. Addressing the elders of the village I informed them of my plan. They were not dismissive. I believed they had admiration for me - for my proposed courage. And the sight of me stomping about with the false leg both amused and impressed them. But they did offer me some help.

When I was ready to leave they brought out the animal. Something like a mule it was. I had not seen such an animal in Upper or su. Across the beast's back they flung a saddle and saddle bags. The saddle was tightened at the girth and a woman began to explain to me how I should tend the beast; how it might feed and more importantly; how I was to ride it. The children laughed at my attempts to mount. The artificial leg did not help me and I fell once. The stump of my leg crushed into the wool and leather. It hurt. Thankfully the beast was mild mannered and patient. I was told later its kind had been bred that way.

Food and grog (throughout Upper and Pandlam/su and "Pangott" people drank grog - but its taste differed from region to region, and so too its strength) was put into the bags and one of the elders gave me an extra fire-piece - old-fashioned but a previous demonstration displayed its effectiveness. And so I mounted the animal one final time and set forth from the village with the children running after me and slapping the poor creature's hind quarters. Luckily for me it still maintained a dignified trot.

It was a curious feeling to be riding a hitherto unknown animal, setting back towards subearth or Pandlam to seek my heavily pregnant wife. It was frightening to think The Catcher too was out there somewhere - and the body of the beautiful Zee. The same Zee whose child was now an orphan; the same Zee on whom I could have laid all my troubles - or my ill-fortune. But also my chance to lead the true life - the true existence – not a sham – not a dag-sham.

A guide had marked a way for me back to the mountain range and a crude map indicated where I might find a pass through the mountains – this was the mountain-pass I had come by - not the pass to the East of the river. The weather was settled and the sun shone in an almost clear cold-blue sky. The tops of the mountains glittered white from fresh falls of snow and yet the meadows and grassy sides were still a rich green. Disease and strife seemed – as they were – a world away.

Forest and woodland covered much of the mountains; icy streams danced down stony causeways. Miniature waterfalls sang to me through the branches of sturdy trees. I inhaled the scent of fresh pine leaves. In the woodlands (lower than the coniferous forests) I had let the animal graze. I gave him a name, this old gentlemen; Eno-luc. This name amused me, and Eno (for short) seemed happy enough with his new title.

Beyond the forests, above their desolate line, was the bleakness of scree and snow. Here there was nothing for Eno to eat and only the sheer magnificent and rugged beauty of the mountains to sustain us. The sun seemed close enough to touch. And the life of Upper as remote as the frozen insects grubbing deep within the hard ground.

I found the pass much easier than I had imagined. But I was surprised how high it was - that I was not spared the fresh falls of snow. How I had forgotten so much of my recent history – and did not recall any of the beautiful – awesome - surroundings. It seemed that only then were my eyes open to what was around me. This struck me so much that I left the mount of Eno and took up some loose rocks and earth with particles of snow-seasoning and scrunched them in my hands. The coldness, the concreteness, the absolute joy of feeling nearly overwhelmed me.

Leading Eno by his rein I limped through the pass between mighty slabs of rock, cleft in two by the brute force of nature. For some time the pass was narrow and the beneficent sun placed in shadow. But slowly the way widened and began to drop and a tremendous vista opened with gentle slopes running down to the valley where the great river ran. I felt like a new man. Like a man who had found *Neumancer*. But it was Pandlam beyond, and beyond that Upper. And what lay beyond Upper? My ignorance was startling. O had I listened well to the Flic-lies. I had wanted to be a good man, and a good man listens well. Listens without duplicity. Perhaps that is why good men are so easily fooled?

Clouds had stolen across part of the sky by then and a light shower brought me to my senses; brought me up sharp. Yet even as the clouds grew black the sun illuminated all.

Then – as I got closer to the river - I saw him.

* * *

The Catcher had reached the riverbank as his beautiful beastie launched itself into the cold waters. What was it to do but continue its pursuit? It knew no danger. It knew only that it had been given a second chance - had felt the love and warmth from its Master's hands. Drank the moistness of its Master's whisperings. With effort the *rath* had clambered down the side of the riverbank and heroically swam against the river's current. But even the will of the Master operating both through its mechanical and organic parts couldn't help it against the flow of nature. And despite its efforts the beastie was carried away to be smashed and rolled by the river's waves – crushed between rocks; savagely washed against earthen and grit banks; folded down beneath the river's cold surface by a strong and inexorable current. To be continually crushed under stone and rock. To be driven to the river's bed and gulped by greedy fish. To have failed! Had it lacked its Master's resolve? Had it been so damaged previously? Were the waters of su, so formidable? Yet if any "life" robotic or organic continued to exist within it - the beastie would struggle on. A fraction of a length a day…for all eternity…

The Catcher could not save it. He sensed the watery spoor of the beastie. Sensed its cries from the white rapids. Sensed that it was being taken far from him - to end where...he knew not. Drowned by eternal waters. But The Catcher had failed once too often. Sitting on the bank he gazed across to the other side. In his right-hand pocket he felt the eyes of Zee. But a pregnant holy-fuck bitch was still out there. He also knew that he had reached the river first. That if he was lucky (but hadn't luck been running out on him for the first time?) he would bag the rebel scum too.

The river flowed and The Catcher waited. Waited until his ageing limbs stiffened. Narrowing his eyes he looked all about him; across to the distant mountains and back in the direction of Wayland. He still had patience and he still was who he was. A messenger, an avenger from the Eloluc. Again he plunged his hand into his pocket and juggled nervously with the eyes of Zee. O, those beautiful eyes.

The girl had put up a brave fight. But he had at least held her alive long enough for him to tell her exactly what he was going to do. And as he exacted each torture upon her he kept her conscious. And each time she endured he told her again, graphically, the nightmares to come. But he could not lie to her. He told her that he had known about Johnny; about the good Doctor Krenz; and that the chains leading from her and them and the transgressor Adam X. would be hauled in and destroyed - link by bloody link. But she heard no news of her baby. And as the final glint of light passed from her eyes she was able to summon one last indignant smile. For her baby was safe. Her baby named Adam lived on. And neither The Catcher nor any of them would ever find out.

The Catcher played with the rifle; the exotic fire-arm. He had brought Zee down with that machine but had finished her in a more primitive fashion; had used the scalpel. Hadn't he communicated with her then? Whispering to her? Letting his sweat mingle with her blood as her life energy drained away. O, what sweetness he had felt.

But in the distance he saw some strange beast approaching. And as he narrowed his glinting eyes he saw a rainbow arc, crossing from the valley of su to the mountains beyond. The sight startled him. Unnerved him. Was that the Bridge? Was it the Bridge that the insane spoke of in subearth? A tingle fired up through the discs of his spine; through the tissue of its column. For if it were the Bridge then was the figure approaching - a strange four-legged beast with two heads - and one the head of a man - the Dark Angel? The Catcher rose and watched the figure grow steadily larger and more detailed. A cloud of dust came from it as if the beast blew fire and smoke. And the beast seemed to have come from the foot of the rainbow; from the end of the Bridge. The Catcher nervously played with the trigger of the rifle. His eyes straining to see.

And then the sun exploded from the clouds with such intensity The Catcher became blinded for some moments; moments that stretched to breaking. And in the blindness he seemed to see the interior of the White Rooms. Seemed to see the fate that awaited us all - not just the little children and the white-bodiers. *The innocents to the slaughter.* And from the whiteness the black figure of the Dark Angel grew steadily closer. The Catcher stepped forward in his blindness and fell into the harsh waters. His rifle slipped from his grasp and plunged below the surface of the river. Desperately he pitched in his arms and hands to fish it out. But still he could not see. Standing then he raised his arms up high as if to shout at the holy-shell manifestation of the Bridge. And then he regained his sight. And he saw the vision "8".

Chapter 20

The sun blinded me as Eno and I approached the great river. A rainbow arched across the sky and filled me with courage. It seemed an auspicious sign spanning Pangott to Pandlam. But in the distance, with my eyes squinting, I could see a dark figure close to the far river bank.

Still astride Eno I kicked the brute's flanks with my one good leg and the artificial stump of the other. Something nagged inside me - it felt as though this was about to be the great ending of all my troubles. To begin with I just sensed an inner vagueness. But as I got closer to the river I realised who the dark figure belonged to. I knew instinctively.

And then I was sure that the final moment had come. I was ready for the finish. Ready to end it all, one way or the other. Ready either to martyr myself or to end the life of an infamous catcher. The sun had dried the thin topsoil of the land and Eno's hooves kicked up a dust. The sun's rays still slanted down as it began its fall to the horizon. Sleet fell over the mountain tops as the clouds blew away. The sun was blinding. Its power dwarfed everything.

Closer we got. The figure seemed to have disappeared for some moments; this could have been the trick of the light, or was the catcher (was it the *real* catcher – *The Catcher*?) also a black magician? And was the beastie about to bite its disease into Eno's legs, bringing him down? Was I to be made the living dead? A zombie? Or killed instantly? But I also thought that there was no sign of Jo. Was she dead already, or had she escaped?

The heaped black mass of clouds gathered over the mountain range behind me. I brought Eno up close to the bank. Across the river the figure of that catcher could see me well enough – and I could see it. I dismounted. The river heaved out white noise.

'Do you know who I am?' I called loudly and boldly across the running waters.

I waited. Watching the figure standing, staring back at me; the hover-cycle behind. Involuntarily I looked about the grass and reeds, half expecting the filth of a *rath* to crawl upon me.

'Do you know who I am?' I called again.

'Yes,' came the voice. A measured, cold, strong voice.

'Do you know what I want?'

He laughed.

'Today I want an end to it all,' I shouted.

'Then come and end it,' the voice jeered. But I detected some grain of fear in that voice - and that I was unprepared for. The voice called to me, 'Do you know who *I* am?'

'You are a catcher – I can see. I know.'

'A catcher?'

'Yes. Scum. A dag-catcher…'

'Brave are you,' he laughed. 'I am not *a* catcher, fool – I am *The Catcher*. The Catcher – do you hear?'

I shivered. The reports had been true. Not just any catcher but the Master of them all. The Catcher. But I was not prepared to show fear - though I felt it deeply. Felt fear deep in my bowels. 'Where is my wife?' I called out bravely.

The figure said nothing.

'Where is the woman known as Jo?'

He laughed. But still did not answer.

'Where is the woman known as Zee?'

'She's watching,' he shouted back.

'You have killed her.'

'She sees from beyond the grave. Come my hunter, my brave angel, come and do battle with the greatest - with a true-life catcher. With *The* Catcher. With he who began it all. Have you the courage to fight me with your will alone?'

I took the fire from one of the packs - it was loaded. The Catcher watched me.

'You fight like a child,' he shouted, 'only a child fights with such toys. Meet me as a man, as an angel, a dark angel, meet me as you are and I as I am; a catcher. If you dare. If you defeat me your woman will be safe - if not I will torture and kill her as I did the holy-slut Zee.' Again he laughed.

The river continued to run between us. It frothed and turned and emitted its relentless white noise.

'And your beasties?' I shouted to him.

The Catcher said nothing for a moment. 'I am alone. My beastie has done its beautiful business. I am in no need of a disease to defeat you...Adam X.' He said my name. I felt chilled by his naming me. There was silence for a moment. Then: 'The disease is already killing you.'

I bit my tongue. I would not tell him yet that I had beaten the disease myself - that my right leg ended in a stump. My trousers hid the wooden shaft of the artificial leg and its rough-hewn shape of a foot rested in my right boot.

'We shall meet in the middle of the river,' The Catcher shouted.

'The middle is too deep, catcher.'

'Do you fear a river, angel?' he bellowed.

'I fear nothing,' I said, and it was true that all fear had indeed left me. I had regained composure. I was prepared.

'Then let it be the middle,' said The Catcher.

I tried not to limp. Was he aware of his advantage? I gritted my teeth and bore the pain of my stump as we both strode into the river's flow. But it became obvious soon enough that The Catcher was allowing me to cross more quickly – though my progress was naturally slower. He waited a third of the way across the river's width. Without much thought I plunged into the icy water and felt its cold numb my mind. Only one foot was able to propel me though I thrust out both legs. With hands swishing about I gulped both water and air. The Catcher seized his moment and waded through the current. I heard his movement above the noise of the water about my ears. I also heard him shout, 'You are a cripple, Adam, a cripple cannot defeat a river and a catcher. I'm going to drown you and then catch your wife. She'll be glad to have a man's whole holy-shell body between her legs.'

He wanted to rile me; to frustrate me. And he succeeded. In my anger I lost control. I "swam" as fast as I could. The river was wide. By the time I stood on the river bed with my head free (and with my artificial leg rested precariously on sand) I was a hopeless target. For the first time I was able to meet his glinting eyes with my own. Saw his determined, furrowed brow. His narrowing eyes focusing on my exposed features. Saw that he was older and thinner than I had imagined. Wading purposefully he got close. His eyes flared. But it was his fist I concentrated on until I blacked my vision. And though I turned my head I still felt its impact as it smashed into my face. Curiously the weight of the water surrounding kept me upright. I lifted my crippled leg and lunged forward.

The Catcher grabbed my hair and began to push down upon my crown. Continuing to lash out with both my legs I gulped frothy water but moved steadily against his body. My might was greater than his and though he kept a tenacious grip on my hair I was able both to gasp in enough air and upset his balance. Again he lashed out with his fists. One of his blows caught my nose and I felt blood trickle down inside. But by then I was above him and able to flash two fingers at his face, jabbing into his eye sockets. He reeled back and, though I was hampered by my leg, I was quickly astride him as both of us sank into the current.

The Catcher kept flaying his arms and lost much energy. I concentrated on keeping him below the water. With difficulty I raised my head enough times to swallow air and spray. But he fought on and caught me between the legs with a water impeded rush of his knee. I thanked the depth of the river. Turning, The Catcher swam back towards his bank. I strode after him as best I could but cursed my limb for its awkwardness. The Catcher turned in shallow water and again I saw the determination in his stare. But I was ready to smash both fists into his face. I watched as he turned his head, still blinking his resolute eyes. He lunged towards me as I let fly two more punches. His nose seemed to splat against his face and a bruise flowered upon his features. Grabbing me by the neck he pulled me close and butted his head against my own. Fortunately he missed the bridge of my nose and our foreheads clattered like goats.

Again I was first to pound his face but he came on relentlessly. Taking hold of my neck he unbalanced me and pushed me under the water. Once I had lost my footing I knew I was in mortal danger. He held on with grim power and I felt the strain on my lungs as I beat my head from side to side. I could feel my lungs close to bursting. Could feel the water ready to rush into my throat and force the life from me. I struggled and kicked but he would not let go. And then the tightness of his grip loosened suddenly. Panicking I pulled his body down beneath the water as I rose and breathed fresh air. Heard the tumult of the river running and saw the blood of The Catcher turn the water about me briefly a deep red.

On the bank, I saw Oomac. Behind him was a shape I almost did not recognise. The sun glinted upon the rippling waters. The Catcher's body floated to the surface and was being taken by the current, downstream. I recognised that shape. And with the sun half-blinding me saw that it was Jo who was being shielded by the rebel.

Before I had time to fully collect my senses and understand what had happened Jo came to the edge of the river bank and slowly made her way into the river. We met knee deep in water and hugged each other. She pushed me away slightly so that the baby was not squashed and looked into my eyes.

'I'm so sorry,' I said.

She said, 'Hush.'

'There's much to explain,' I began.

'We have time,' she smiled.

Looking at her eyes I could see that she had changed, had undergone hardships equal to mine in their own way. I knew what she had wanted from me and our life together and yet by some bizarre connections of fate she was standing in a river, heavily pregnant, close to the border of a country only months previously she wouldn't have believed existed.

We struggled to the river bank and between myself and Oomac helped Jo back out. I hugged Oomac and thanked him for delivering my wife to me - and for shooting The Catcher dead.

'It seemed I couldn't do it on my own,' I said.

'You'unt needed help,' he beamed.

Jo hadn't taken her eyes off my leg then, as if she had genuinely only just realsied. The bottom of my trousers were ripped and she could see wood where flesh should have been.

Looking at her I said, 'It's not so bad...could have been worse.'

She nodded. After a moment's pause she said coolly, 'I know about Zee.'

'Yes,' I said softly.

'Many have died,' said Oomac; many more will I am afraid. But wese will do our bit for a free Pandlam. And to set Upper free too.'

Jo looked at me.

'Seems we all need liberating,' I said. Then I lay on the ground in utter exhaustion.

The sun still shone in the sky as we talked and ate. Even Eno braved the water and joined us on our side.

Jo told me of her adventure. Of her change of heart towards...towards myself and all the trouble I had heaped upon her and us. But there was nuance in her speech, which led me to believe that what had happened she understood to be for the best. That at least we were free. Poor. But free. And we did not have the disease.

Oomac wished us well as I led Eno back across the river with Jo sitting uncomfortable and side-saddle. Once on the Pangott bank I turned to wave to the rebel leader but he had disappeared into the distance.

'He is a great man,' Jo said.

'We have a long way to go,' I said.

'Yes.'

'We have much to learn,' I said.

'And we've begun,' she answered.

'Let the moon show his evil face,' I whispered.

Jo looked at me but said nothing.

On our way towards the mountains I decided that the child would be born at the village and when we three were strong enough we would set forth for the uncharted territory deeper within the mystery lands. I held my wife's hand as we made steady time.

That night we slept together under the stars. Kept each other warm beneath a heavy blanket. I tried to tell her things; tell about why I had done what I'd done and how things had developed since my absence...but again she hushed me. Again told me that we had time.

Once I awoke to hear her gentle sobbing in the night. Her sacrifice to freedom was far greater than mine.

The End

Two whole sequences of seasons later and we are here in a beautiful land the equal of *Neumancer*; the equal of anything that can be dreamt. Life is hard but real. We have been joined by some from the village who also followed our dreams of freedom and truth. Our child, little Oomac, is strong and healthy. My wife is pregnant again and I am sure it will be a baby girl. If it is so we have decided she will be called Zee. It is the measure of love Jo has for me. Because it is true that Zee led us to this place - I listened to her whisperings on the breezes of the New World.

We are blissfully happy. We struggle to survive. We feel the rhythms of nature. We hunt, we gather and with seeds brought by the new ones we intend to grow crops. We have befriended a wild dog. We have been given a second chance. It is a life as far removed from Upper – and subearth – as is possible. I still recall my life and continue to tell its tale and incorporate Jo's adventures. I still remember the moment I became aware of the disease – of the time when I severed the flesh and bone of my own leg. Of the death of The Catcher.

Today Jo and I walked to the edge of a great hilltop and looked into the farthest distance.

'That is our future,' I said to her.

'Ours and our children's,' she replied.

I will write down our history, all of the adventures that befell me and hear more of what happened to Jo. One day both our children; Oomac and little Zee will read what I have written and then they too will add to the narrative. One day maybe Adam – born into the world of Upper – will hear the call in the distance on a wild, stormy night and reject the sham dag world of Upper and seek out a new life in a new land. Maybe one day we will track him down and a helper will whisper strange words to him.

Soon I will take my son to the edge of this hill and then I will hold him aloft and say quietly, 'Oomac, this land does not belong to you but you shall be its guardian. With the blessing of the land you will be free. Free. Live truthfully, my son and freedom will be bestowed upon you. Remember who you are, where you came from but keep your eye on the far horizon. Be strong. Be free.'

And after all that has befallen myself, my wife and family, and those who died I contemplate the Life Code:

We exist; we maintain the Laws of Nature; we increase (isn't it so?); we know our own boundary - for it is limitless. But we do not credate. Alas (!) the oubliette is denied us. We are our own people, answerable to none. But there is one pursuit I must add to the code of Upper, and it is the one pursuit I will strive for throughout our new life.

Freedom

Biting Tongues

Available from www.lulu.com/blackcatsite

This is the story of Jack "Jackie" who has been imprisoned in an old air-raid shelter for seven years and seven months. The novel begins with Jackie's diary extracts written from within a mental hospital. The story is about why Jack was imprisoned and the effect of that imprisonment on him and all those connected.

Biting Tongues conjures the experience of those who have dwelt in another world within our world – an "oubliette" – and who, when they are released back into "reality", are looked to for insight and wisdom. It is as if their suffering and isolation can give us the answers we seek to the meaning of our collective (and relatively safe) existence.

The novel investigates Jack's "dream-time" which he learnt to enter in "the dark" as he terms it. "Dream-time" is about the transformation of thoughts into words and words into "reality". This is mirrored by his obsession with books in the hospital and in this sense the novel explores the relationship between reality and fiction (and the creative act) – plus the redemptive power of fiction.

In the dark, Jack had to learn to survive.

The main themes are: love; time; the nature of sanity/insanity; freedom and imprisonment; redemption; power. The main sub-plot of the novel deals with how and why Jack is imprisoned.

Against all the anguish of the past there is a movement of optimism and for all the bitterness and darkness in this novel there is also a powerful sense of love and hope.

It is Jack's imprisonment and the strange world of twilight reality enmeshed with dream-time fiction that gives the whole novel its peculiar feeling and narrative direction.

- [this is] very well written…[and] shows great talent and originality – Susan Mears

- [writing that is] precise and eminently readable, the dialogue unaffected and plausible…there is much to admire – Jonathan Butler

Tim Bragg writes fast-paced literary fiction. *Biting Tongues* is published by Black Cat Distribution (2005) while *Veneer; Seeds and The Corridor* are pending publication. In 2001 he had a novel *The English Dragon* published (Athelney; www.athelney.org) – he has written a sequel to this titled *Oak* (to be published in 2006). He has also written two genre novels – a thriller, *ONX* and a sci-fi horror novel, *The White Rooms* (Black Cat Distribution 2005).
Over the past decade he has had many short-stories published in magazines, won literary prizes and had poetry and articles published too. He is a singer-songwriter, plays guitar and flute and "gigs" regularly playing drums with a jazz band. Married to a French woman he has a young son.
Biting Tongues (in an earlier first draft) was championed by Alice Thomas Ellis; the opening of Veneer was recently read and described thus:
It's absolutely FABULOUS!! There is so much "power" in it. It's a long time since I have read a book with such intensity. What I find thrilling about this novel is its whole process; the way the narrative reads so well. You write in a very rich language; but it's not the sort of rich language some poets use – a "baroque" style full of curls and curves - it's rich and plain, sweet and sour at the same time – it's very deep - Michaela Vejvodova.

Printed in Great Britain
by Amazon

58951834R00103